The Curly Collection
Colleen Noonan

 Busybird Publishing
2/118 Para Road, Montmorency Victoria 3094
www.busybird.com.au

First published by Busybird Publishing and Design 2012
Reprinted 2017

Copyright © 2012 Colleen Noonan
e: colleen.noonan10@bigpond.com

Cover Image & illustrations: Colleen Noonan
Layout and Design: Blaise van Hecke

ISBN 978 0 9871538 7 6

Typeset in Garamond 12pt

THE CURLY COLLECTION
Colleen Noonan

The following pages are devoted to the dilemmas confronting
my good mate Curly. Curly is ordinary. Yet perhaps hoping,
like all of us, to one day be extraordinary. But first and
foremost he is a 'writer'. For this reason alone, I can equate
with my unlikely hero. I hope that you can too!

The Curly Collection first evolved in the year 2011 when I
joined the Diamond Valley Living & Learning
'Write your Stories' Group.

With special thanks to the following for your ongoing
encouragement and support
my first friend in writing, Noelene Goodwin
teachers, Kay Arthur and Liz Mildenhall
publisher, Blaise van Hecke
Paul Dunell, without whom I never would have gotten started,
Lyn, Gwen, Joanne, Nikki, Claudia, Gwenda, Veronica, Jill,
Giovanna, Peter, Jane, Natasha and
'the Larrikin', who convinced me from day one to continue
with the development of my character, Curly.

For my family
Lisa, Wade, Eugene, Julie,
William, Mackenzie, Henry, Archer
and my most valued critic
Bill
Love Always

MMM
✝

Contents

Morning Writing

'I've picked up some sort of a bug,' Curly O'Callahan warned his dog Shakespeare.

'Don't come too close fella. Y' just never know ... it could be contagious!'

Shakespeare's ears were pricked, and his tail thumped up and down on the floor creating a draft. He sat perfectly alert, leant his head to one side and looked with an expression of confusion upon the weary face of his master.

Curly was seated on the edge of the bed scratching his head, yawning and sliding his feet inside a pair of fleecy lined slippers.

'Maybe it's an infection!' he added.

'Nope ... come to think of it ... more likely an addiction! Whatever you might like to call it Shakes, there's not a doubt in me mind that ... writin' ... once it gets int' y' blood, is a serious affliction from which it seems impossible to recover. A bloke can't get a decent night's sleep anymore, in between worryin' about carbon tax, the bloody possums and the writin'!'

Morning, afternoon, evening ... whose keeping count really! All Curly knew was that the sun no longer rises, or sets, without having jotted down a few lines to either complete his latest short story or round out a further chapter of his novel. Suddenly, it would seem that writing had taken precedence over all sorts of things he would have once considered to be of far greater importance.

'Surely this can't be normal Shakes? Crikey ... do y' s'pose I've got a touch of the Jeffrey Archer's mate?' Shakespeare looked curious. Or maybe been hit with the Bryce Courtenay stick! Of course ... at this rate, a bloke could be famous! The two of us might be dinin' on caviar f' brekkie ol' son, once I make the bestseller list. Writin' stretches the brain box I reckon ... havin' t' come up with imaginative ideas every day of y' life. It's bloody hard work mate!'

The dog gave a low whining yawn in agreement, seeming happy to be consulted about the matter, and padded closely behind Curly's heels as he wandered into the next room to turn on the computer.

'Okay Shakes, let's go 'n boil up the billy.'

Moments later, they returned from the kitchen and Curly seated himself in front of the screen crunching on a bowl of cereal. Shakespeare settled into the corner and with a forlorn sigh rested his chin on his front paws, then lifted his eyes mournfully.

'No good lookin' at a bloke like that Shakes, I promise to take y' for a walk later. Just need t' get a few thoughts down on paper. We writers are artistes you realise and must work when the mind is fresh and focused.'

Sipping a mug of tea, Curly felt a certain sense of guilt as he placed the hot steaming liquid carefully down on the desktop. Supposing he should accidentally upend the contents and ruin the computer? He'd been harshly disciplined about this very situation many times in the past. Supposing someone should knock on the door to find him dishevelled and unshaven. And supposing both he and Shakespeare grew lethargic and unfit due to a lack of fresh air and exercise. It's a trap! A writer's dilemma! But one that he no longer seemed to have sufficient willpower to avoid.

Curly's plan to simply check out the emails and shut down, failed on every occasion. A couple of hours would pass by and he'd find himself positioned in exactly the same spot to suddenly look up at the clock in disbelief, 'No ... I've done it again Shakes! Wasted the entire morning.'

Well this had certainly not been his intention today. After all, it was his holiday break and everyone knows that the best thing to do during a holiday is to wind down so that the body and mind has a chance to regenerate. It's a time to sit back and relax and let the Easter Bunny do all of the hard yakka. It's a time to eat hot cross buns and chocolate eggs. Everyone knows that.

But eagerly, with hands poised like those of a concert pianist over the keyboard, Curly realized that his desire to write was both stronger and far more urgent than the need to take stock of his nagging addiction. What's the point in trying to fight it! Surely, there could be no harm in taking just a few more minutes to briefly gather up some thoughts on the subject of how much he had always loved Easter. And especially the mellow crisp season of autumn. So, despite his former good intentions, Curly proceeded ...

Several hours later as Curly and Shakespeare finally wandered off into the distance on their delayed morning walk, the *writing bug* followed. Hence the mystery being still left unsolved. Did Curly O'Callahan really wish to be rid of this so called affliction which now seemed destined to remain a part of his life forever?

Maybe Shakespeare is the only one who will ever truly know the answer!

The Right Colour

Many years ago, Curly could recall one of his favourite television shows in which a sad little frog sang a song entitled "it's not that easy bein' green". Kermit thought that he was ordinary and just blended in with the world around him. He was the colour of the leaves and wanted, like all of us, to stand out and make a bold statement.

Curly O'Callahan had lived his entire life wondering if he would ever stand out. His mate, Smudge and dog Shakespeare seemed to think he was okay, but what about the rest of the world?

Yet Curly had always admired Kermit, and at the time could remember thinking he was misguided, and had longed to reassure him as to the belief in the beauty of his own colour. 'Don't be so unhappy!' he would have willingly told him. 'Stop complainin' and singing that mournful tune filled with self doubt and pity.' But it's difficult to chastise a muppet who thinks he's really a frog, even if he is in need of counselling.

Curly supposed if he were asked his own favourite colour, the answer would most definitely be green. But Kermit would probably conclude 'that's easy for you to say Curly O'Callahan ... but see how you might feel if you were to awaken one morning to find your condition permanent!'

He did have a point, and lately Curly had been feeling a bit low himself. Even Shakes had been looking down in the mouth. So he decided that perhaps he should call Smudge to discuss the matter.

'G'day mate ... whatcha up to?' Curly asked.

'A bloke's just sittin' here tryin' to quietly read "the paper." But that won't last for long mate. Shaz has already been on me back wantin' me to mow the lawn. Why ... what can I do for ya ol' son?'

'Smudge, you've known me a long time. Nearly all me life, in fact. Do ya reckon that I stand out?'

'What are y' talkin' about Curly?'

'Well ... do I make a bold statement? I mean ... in a crowd, and all that, mate?'

'To tell y' the truth Curly, I don't think you leave anyone in much doubt of your feelin's when we go to the footy. You're a bloody embarrassment mate!'

'No, no ... y' got me meanin' all wrong Smudge. What I'm askin' is, well ... have I got ... well, you know ...'

'Geez Curly, stop beatin' about the bush. Out with it mate! I haven't got all bloody day ya know.'

`Pa ... Panache!' Curly stammered. 'You know Smudge ... s'pose it's a bit like savoir faire!'

'Blimey ... you should give away that writin' mate, it's affectin' y' brain. Savie-wa ... who? Y' can't be bloody serious. You've got me well and truly stumped on providin' the correct answer to that one. A bloke's not a walkin' encyclopedia ya know. But then o' course, on the other hand, there's no denyin' the one thing ya have got plenty of, and that's bloody per ... nash mate. Anyone will tell ya that.'

'Do y' really think so Smudge? Y' not just pullin' me leg to make me feel better, are ya?'

'Would ya bloody best mate try 'n pull the wool over y' eyes? When it comes to pernash Curly O'Callahan ... mate ... you're right up there at the top of the list.'

'Gee, thanks Smudge.

'Not a doubt in me mind Curly ol' son. There's absolutely no question about it!'

Once Curly had gotten off the phone, Smudge looked puzzled and said to his wife Sharon.

'Ya know what Shaz, I worry about ol' Curly sometimes. That was him askin' me if he's got pernash. And aw yeah ... some other sort o' French soundin' disease.'

'Pernash!' said Sharon.

'That's right luv.

'What the hell is pernash?'

'Well that's just the point ... I've really got no idea luv!'

Curly felt so much better as he knew he could always rely on his mate Smudge whenever he needed an honest answer. And then he felt even more relieved to remember that Kermit had eventually gone on to discover the truth as well. It really wasn't so bad bein' green because it is the colour of Spring. Kermit's career blossomed and he grew into a big star proving, just like Curly, that he didn't need a therapist. Life is simply about accepting your own particular colour and never fogetting just how truly special it is. Curly bent down to pat Shakespeare and reassured him – 'Shakes, you've just gotta keep believing in y'rself. After all that Smudge is a pretty smart fella!'

The Rounds Of The Kitchen

'Geez Curly, you look a bit buggered mate!'

'Nothin' that a coupla cold beers won't fix I reckon Smudge.'

'Have you been sittin' up all night writin' again?'

Curly looked guilty.

'Y' know what the problem is don't ya ol' son?'

'What problem's that Smudge?'

'I reckon you've become a slave to that computer o' yours. It's dominatin' ya life Curly. Y' need t' get out in the sunshine mate and get some vitamin D int' y' system. Y're as pale as one o' them poor-sel-lane dolls. Even me backside's got more colour than your face mate ... 'n that never sees the light o' day either.'

'Come off it Smudge! There's no need to be crass mate.'

'What the hell are y' writin' anyway Curly ... the bloody mag-nee-a carta mate?'

'Pass me the chips will ya Smudge!'

'These'r ... these are salt 'n vinegar! I've told y' before, ya shouldn't be eatin' this rubbish.'

'Knock it off Smudge ... they were on special. Two f' the price o' one!'

'Surely y're a wake up t' that caper. That's just t' get ya t' spend more dough mate.'

'Y're beginnin' t' sound like me mum Smudge!'

'You've gotta start takin' betta care of y'self ol' son, or ... fair dinkum, one of these days you'll cark it. It's that simple mate! An' I f' one don't relish the thought of carryin' ya outa that computer room o' yours, feet first with ya hands still stuck frozen to the keyboard. I'll have t' prize the two of ya apart before they can bury ya mate.'

'Pass me the chips will ya Smudge!'

'No point tryin' t' change the subject. I'm a wake up t' that caper as well Curly O'Callahan. You mark my words mate, y' need to get out 'n about a bit more. Maybe even consider goin' on a date!'

'Strewth! At my age Smudge. Y' gotta be kiddin' me.'

'What about that ah ... what's 'er name again ... aw yeah ... that "Penny-lope"? The sheila you were tellin' me about the other day.'

'Aw ... come off it Smudge ... a bloke's not that desperate. An' anyway, her name's not "Penny-lope" it's "Penelope" y' stupid fool. Y' know ... like that movie star that used t' go out with "Tom Cruise". Besides ... she wouldn't give an ol' bugger like me the time o' day mate.'

'Well ... excuse me ol' son! But, with the greatest respect Curly, ya do understand that she wouldn't be considered a lot o' blokes' cup a tea with a name like "Penelope."'

'Tom Cruise didn't seem to find it a problem Smudge. In fact, I think he even married the woman.'

'Forget about "Tom Cruise" mate. That's how he makes a livin' ... bein' an actor 'n all. He gets paid to speak Spanish. We're talkin' "Curly O'Callahan" here. There's a bit of a difference ya know.'

'"Penelope's" not a Spanish name Smudge.'

'Well that maybe so Curly. But a name like that ... well it's got it's limitations I reckon. There's no denyin' it's a bit of a bloody mouthful.' Now you take my missus f' instance. A good solid name "Shaz". As pure as the day is long. That's what y' need Curly. What are the blokes at the pub gunna think if ya turn up with some bird called "Penny-lope" in tow? I'll tell ya what they'll think mate, "Geez that Curly O'Callahan's gettin' a bit high 'n bloody mighty."'

'Well ... that'd be their problem Smudge!'

'Maybe she'd let y' shorten it ... I mean once ya got t' know 'er a bit! P'rhaps "Nell" might be the go. Yeah, that should appeal to you bein' a writer 'n all. Another good solid name o' sorts.

Or, on second thoughts, even ... just plain "Pen". Every writer needs a pen! Aw ... come on Curly, give 's a bit of va grin for Christ's sake. Ya losin' y' sense o' humour as well ol' son!'

'Ya wastin' y' time Smudge. An' as I'm not plannin' on gettin' t' know 'er any better, I can't really see it bein' a problem, 'n that's the bloody end of it.'

'Okay! No point gettin' upset about somethin' that may not eventuate. But if ya haven't come good by the next time I see ya Curly, I'm gunna take ya out on a date m'self. An' that's a promise mate!'

Once Smudge had left, Curly thought about all these years he'd lived on his own. Sure there'd been a few girlfriends along the way, but only one that he'd ever really wanted to marry.

Shakespeare wandered across the room and nudged his wet nose into the palm of Curly's hand.

'You understand me ... don't ya pal? And I wouldn't want ya to take any notice of this date business that Smudge is on about. There'll be no woman comin' between the two of us interferin' 'n takin' over our lives. I've got a book t' write and we need our independence!'

Shakespeare's tail wagged playfully and Curly's pale face suddenly looked a whole lot brighter.

Japan – 2011

Michael Leunig, the cartoonist, once depicted a state of depression so simply in a drawing of the little big nosed man from Curly Flat. Mr. Curly starts out his morning in high spirits appearing perfectly happy and content.

Curly O'Callahan whistled as he gathered up his notepad and pen, and eagerly set off in the sunshine to attend his first writing class. All was going well, until ...

'Homework ... hmm ... think maybe you should write about Japan,' suggested the teacher of Curly's newly formed group.

Oh no ... anything but Japan! he thought.

Then the news was to get worse.

'Perhaps a story about an Aussie working in Tokyo when the tsunami hits.'

This lady really knows how to dampen a bloke's enthusiasm. Curly sighed.

Of all the topics one could choose, this would be by far the most disturbing. Surely everybody's worst nightmare! A nightmare, which for so many, became a seemingly impossible reality. Curly wandered away in disappointment.

Given that, unlike the poor souls in Japan, Curly should be granted some sort of reasonable control and choice over the matter – he'd promised himself at the beginning of this brand new year that his days would be filled with a positive and far more uplifting approach to life. And throughout the following months, he'd become even more determined to remain true to this promise when constantly reminded that everything could change in a minute. Not only as a result of ill health, but also, as so recently demonstrated, due to a freak act of nature.

Having never been to Japan, Curly would find it tremendously difficult to comment about what life might be like living in Tokyo. Yet he supposed it could be argued that the definition of a good writer is someone who is able to relate any story. So reluctantly, he turned his mind to the terror of working inside a swaying city office block skyscraper, imagining his desperation when uncertain if the entire building might suddenly plummet to the ground, collapsing like a pack of cards. Or perhaps be swallowed up into the deep dark abyss of the unstable earth presently located some umpteen floors beneath his feet.

Shuddering in horror, Curly thought that if there'd been one lesson that he'd learnt the hard way throughout his lifetime, it was to never dwell on those matters, which leave a person feeling totally miserable. The longer one wallows in unhappiness or self pity, the easier it is to become disillusioned and dispirited inviting, or even encouraging, the symptoms of depression or physical illness.

As the hours progress, Mr. Curly ponders over all of the worldly problems confronting him throughout the day and gradually becomes weighed down by the worrisome burden created by so much bad news.

It's difficult to comprehend how fickle is the unleashed anger of the Gods. And how insignificant the people and animals when trampled upon, crushed and drowned like ants. As a lover of fairytales Curly thought, it's as though a giant Gulliver has been ever so careless about where he might place his feet or clumsily upturn his brimming soup bowl. But, unlike a fairytale, there was no happy ending. For those thousands of victims who resided along the fishing villages, one minute living their complex or simple lives, maybe some attending a writing class such as himself - how little their hopes and dreams all seemed to matter.

Curly would pray each day to a gentler God, a much more compassionate God, for all the homeless survivors. Curly would pray for those in distress who unlike the visitor, have no means of escape. For those who remain, destined to suffer this grave situation exposed to the radiation whilst fearful as to the terrifying consequences of tomorrow. And finally, Curly would pray for his own self preservation and that of his loved ones, neighbours and countrymen in a world that seems constantly threatened by the deadly forces of nature, which indiscriminately kill, leaving behind a trail of misery and destruction.

By nightfall Mr. Curly's once upright posture is slumped and weary. With drooping shoulders and downcast eyes his cheerful demeanour has turned to gloom, his face forlorn and filled with an expression of sadness and despair.

With the task completed, Curly O'Callahan sat back and quietly read through his story. There was little doubt that this subject still weighed heavily on his mind. Yet surprisingly, the need to write had proved far greater than the need to bury his head in the sand. Curly had learnt an important lesson. The challenge of producing a story to which initially he'd been so strongly opposed, had stretched his imagination and introduced him to a world where nothing would ever again seem impossible.

Show Not Tell

'What have you got behind y' back there Curly?' Smudge asked.

'Well it's a secret Smudge. I really can't *tell* ya.'

'If you can't *tell* me, then you'll just have to *show* me now won't cha!'

'What about if you were to close your eyes and let me describe exactly what I'm hidin'. If you can guess what it is ... then it's yours mate.'

'Sounds a bit childish Curly. What's the catch?'

'It's just an exercise f' me writin' class. An experiment you might say. But maybe just to be on the safe side, so that there'll be no cheatin' or anythin', it might be betta if I was t' blindfold ya. Not t' say that I don't completely trust ya ol' son.'

'Go ahead then Curly! There's no way that y' can trick an intelligent bloke such as meself.'

'Okay Smudge. Now the idea is that I'm going to *show* you by the power of descriptive words exactly what I have behind me back. It must become so real and vivid inside y' mind that you can see it as though it were right in front of your eyes. Are y' ready?'

'Go f' it Curl!'

'Behind me back is a rectangular shaped object.'

'Blimey that rules out a can of VB mate!'

'It has a timber frame around the perimeter over which is stretched a colourful canvas.'

'Aw ... y' must think a bloke's a bit of a goose. You've got one of them paintin's behind y' back. I win it's all over ol' son. What game do ya wanna play next?'

'That's absolutely correct Smudge. Of course it's not an original ... only a smaller reproduction you understand. But that's the easy part. You must now determine precisely what you see as ya view the painting and *tell* me the name of this familiar scene without me revealin' the answer.'

'Come off it Curly ... that's unfair. Y' know that I know nothin' about artwork.'

'I think everyone is familiar with this one Smudge. The paintin' has depth and perspective.'

'Geez Curly, speak in a language I can understand, will ya mate. What in the bloody hell is perspective?'

'Well that means you can see from close up, back into the distance. The colours are of a rich sepia shade in keepin' with the times and the timber surroundin's depicted in the settin'. There are also touches of blue and pale orange.'

'But what's actually in the bloody pitcha mate?'

'There are quite a few blokes in the busy scene Smudge.'

'No women!' Smudge replied in disgust. 'Well this also rules out that what's 'is name "Lindsay." Yeah "Norman Lindsay" if I recollect correctly ... the bloke who painted all them naked sheilas with the big bums mate. Not sure that he knew a whole lot about perspective either Curly!'

'Forget about nude women will ya Smudge. To the right of the picture there squats a bloke with a long white beard leanin' against the wall. He's wearin' what looks like one of them safari hats. Y' know Smudge a pith helmet, and he seems to be keepin' a close eye on watchin' the workers.'

'Is he the boss then Curly?'

'Don't think so mate. He's dressed in a pale blue shirt and dark blue vest and I reckon he'd have to be the foreman overseein' the work. And to the left of the picture is a young lad, carryin' a fleece. Directly behind him another slightly older strappin' lookin' young bloke is standin' at the entrance of what appears to be a holdin' pen, draggin' a ram which he's got a firm upright grip of in his arms. In the central foreground we see the first in a line of shearers bent over the sheep toilin' with his clippin' shears, and the scene is repeated all the way back to the rear of the shearin' shed.'

'I've got it in one mate. You were right ... even I know Tom Roberts "Shearin' the Rams." Me absolute favourite. It's a corka that paintin'!' Smudge flung off his blindfold. 'I love this pitcha Curly.'

'Well consida it a gift fer y' birthday mate. But I'm still a bit confused Smudge.'

'Why's that Curly?'

'Well I can't say that the difference between *show 'n tell* is all that clear to me even though you guessed the right answer. But I think it may be betta not to mention it to anyone else in me writin' class or they might consider me to be a bit of a drongo mate.'

Tools Of The Trade

Curly stumbled in through the back door, carrying several awkwardly shaped shopping bags, and dropped them with a heavy sigh of relief onto the kitchen floor.

'Well Shakes,' he gestured, 'a bloke should be guaranteed to have the whole box and dice inside these bags ... the tools of the trade so t' speak. No expense has been spared. Y' see it doesn't matter what type o' job a bloke attempts in this life – it makes all the difference having exactly the right equipment. Me ol' man taught me that when I was just a kid. "As y' go through life Curly me boy," he said, "remember this advice and you'll never have a worry in the world about being a success mate." A very knowledgeable fella was me ol' dad y' know Shakes!'

Like a flamboyant magician, from within the depths of a large plastic bag, Curly then theatrically whipped out a parcel, ripped away the wrapping and flung it into the air. Shakespeare was hoping to discover a fluffy white rabbit that he could chase around the kitchen, but to his disappointment, the only item that Curly revealed was a small Teflon pan.

Shakespeare, being not quite certain as to Curly's intentions, grew slightly nervous as his master proudly waved the pan around in the air with a flourish. And taking several steps backwards, he sat at a safer distance to study these unusual antics.

For several seconds Curly scrutinized his new pan turning it this way and that. `Shakespeare ol' son ... allow me to introduce you to this perfectly sized stovetop pan. This is not just any old pan I hope you realise Shakes. This is no flash in the pan. This is a magic pan which shall enable me, one Curly O'Callahan, masterchef extraordinaire, to prove to Smudge that the writer within has yet another string to his bow. For in this pan which you now see before you, I shall endeavour to produce the perfect French crepe. Not only that my boy ... '

Curly paused and once again reached down inside the rattling bag before withdrawing a further mystery object disguised in bubble wrap.

'But here ... you would also be well advised to cast your eye over a perfectly formed enamel jug. An essential item Shakes from which to pour the all important liquid ingredients.'

Shakespeare had never seen Curly acting so strangely or speaking in such an odd manner. He was a little confused and now slinked into the corner thinking that he much preferred the old plain Curly the writer, as opposed to this new Curly, the Masterchef. And whilst continuing to line up his goodies, Curly then went on to inform Shakespeare of the menu planned for Smudge's upcoming celebration.

'F'r the entree, I shall prepare a simple paté, followed by a richly flavoured, heartwarmin' French casserole Shakes – *Coq au Vin*. Accompanied by a loaf of crusty white bread. And lastly, the mouth waterin' dessert of delicious *Crepes Suzette* served with a dollop of thickened cream.'

Shakespeare licked his lips and thought longingly of the tasty leftovers.

Curly had spent hours thumbing through the pages of an outdated edition of the Australian Women's Weekly cookbook, determined to find a dinner party recipe to suit his exacting requirements. He was a romantic at heart, and although his culinary skills were fairly limited, he didn't need much convincing that the ol' French cuisine, coupled with the right drop of wine and a touch of candlelight, would be difficult to surpass when it came to the art of fine dining.

Curly slipped a trendy new apron over his head and flicked through his brand new recipe book which contained simple step-by-step instructions as to *the secret of cooking the perfect crepe*. Next he produced a heavy black cast iron pan which fitted snugly over a small burner that sat in the centre of an impressive copper tray.

'And here we have the pi-ace de resistonce ... me tabletop flambay-er Shakes. Imagine ol' Smudge's face when I fire this thing up right under his nose! And aw yeah ... I almost forgot ... an authentic Bendigo pottery casserole dish in which to slow cook the *Coq au Vin*. Voila!' He lifted the lid and sniffed inside as though the chicken was already cooked and just out of the oven. `Magnifique! What do ya reckon Shakes?'

Shakespeare responded with a slight whimper, but couldn't even begin to imagine what all the fuss was about.

Curly was aware that Smudge, being somewhat lacking in culture, would probably be the first to disagree with all of this unfamiliar and rather lavish French opulence. But Curly O'Callahan had carefully considered the menu and made his decision. There would be no turning back.

A Toast To Smudge

Still wearing his apron, Curly's face was beaming when he opened the front door to greet his two guests. He shook Smudge by the hand and suavely kissed Shaz on each cheek as he'd seen Gerard Depardieu do in those foreign French movies.

'Geez Curly, don't go oversteppin' the mark with a bloke's Missus there ol' son. It's not her Birthday y' know.'

'Aw ... be quiet luv. Curly's just bein' polite.'

'Is that what ya bloody call it. Coulda fooled me! I would o' thought he's takin' a few unnecessary liberties meself.'

'For God's sake Smudge, put a sock in it will you!'

'Only havin' a bit of fun luv.' Smudge laughed giving Shaz a friendly pat on the backside. 'Well go on ... in ya go outa the cold. Bloody hell Curly, has the power gone off ... why's the place in darkness? A bloke can't see his nose in front of his face in 'ere. Strike a light, what's with the candles an' all them balloons coverin' up the whole of the bloody ceilin' mate!'

'Shuddup will y' Smudge. Can't you see that Curly's gone to a lot of trouble making the house look special. Sometimes you've got no class. I think the room is lovely Curly, you must have been workin' for a month of Sundays luv!'

'It was nothin' really Shaz.'

Shakespeare nudged his nose affectionately into Smudge's hand.

'G'day Shakes. I didn't see ya there in the dark. How's it goin' pal?'

Shakespeare lifted his paw to Shaz.

'Nice to see you too Shakes,' Shaz said taking his paw and giving him a playful pat on the head.

'Curly me ol' mate ... this here bein' such a special celebration 'n all, I've brought along a little bottle of somethin' to wet ya whistle. F' starters how about we down a coupla of pre-dinner savy-non blonks, and to mix in with the horse's doovas you might like to add these salt 'n vinegar chips which I know to be ya favourite. T' help out with the cookin', Shaz here, has whipped up a few of them lamingtons ya love so much.'

'That's very thoughtful of ya both, considerin' I told y' not to worry about bringin' anythin'.

'Think nothin' of it Curly. It's the least a mate can do, in appreciation of the chef havin' slaved over a hot stove all day. Me 'n Shaz have been really lookin' forward to sittin' down t' enjoy a home cooked dinner of roast lamb ... haven't we luv?'

A Toast To Smudge

'Well I hope ya not gunna be too disappointed Smudge, but seein' as this is no ordin'ry run o' the mill occasion, I've cooked up a French dish for a change.'

'That's a bit disappointin' mate. I hope y' not expectin' Shaz and meself to eat them bloody snails y' been complainin' about recently f' wreckin' ya vegie garden.'

'I'm sure whatever Curly's got planned for dinner, it will be very tasty Smudge. It certainly smells delicious!'

Curly poured his guests their first drink and carried a large box into the lounge room, placing it squarely at Smudge's feet.

'This is y' present mate ... from Shakes and meself.'

'Hey, what's this all about Curl? You've already given a bloke the paintin'. Shaz and I have worked out the perfect spot for it, haven't we luv? It's gunna take pride o' place right over the top of the Rinnai gas heater.'

'Well let's just say this is somethin' a little extra from Shakes for all the times that you an' Shaz have taken him in whenever I've needed ya. It's almost like his second home at your place.'

'That's very good of ya Curly ol' son and o' course Shakes 'ere is always a welcome guest. I was only pullin' y' leg before. I'm really grateful to ya f' all this effort you've gone to decoratin' the house and cookin' up a special dinner 'n all.'

'Aw ... that's okay Smudge ... glad y' like it mate!'

Smudge tore off the wrapping to discover a slab of VB and a jar of salted beer nuts.

'Geez ya really know how t' spoil a bloke Curly. These'll hit the right spot and keep me goin' f' a night or two. Thanks ol' son.'

Shakespeare wagged his tail, grabbed the wrapping paper and did a lap out through the dining room, into the kitchen and back into the lounge room, then dropped the crumpled paper right at Smudge's feet.

'Of course, I couldn't forget me other best pal ... thanks Shakes. You and Curly are like me own flesh 'n blood.'

Smudge dug deep inside his pocket, pulled out a hankie and loudly blew his nose.

'Well I think the guest of honour should be seated at the head of the table. You sit in the middle here Shaz,' Curly directed as he carefully pulled out her chair.

'The table looks so nice Curly,' Shaz commented.

'Y' may have t' dispense with them flowers though brother. I reckon they might start affectin' me nasal passages. Ya know how me sinus-ses play up on me.'

'No worries Smudge, I'll just put them over here outa the way. Shaz, are you plannin' to stick to the champagne cocktails ... cause if you're happy with that, I've got a bottle of red to share between me 'n Smudge here.'

'I'll be dancing on the table if I have any more of this bubbly Curly.'

'Give 'er another one mate. It's Saturd'y night and we could do with a few laughs. Maybe if you were t' whip the shade off that tall lamp you've got sittin' over there Curly, Shaz might do a bit o' that erotic pole dancin' those sheilas get up to at them sleazy nightclubs.'

'For God's sake Smudge, how on earth do you know what sheilas do at the nightclubs?'

'I've seen them shimmyin' up and down them poles on the tele o' course.' Smudge winked at Curly.

Curly decided it might be a whole lot safer to stay right out of this discussion, and busied himself pouring the wine and serving the paté.

'Well I think we should raise our glasses Shaz, and toast ol' Smudge here on his birthday. Happy birthday mate and bon appetit-o.'

Smudge swirled the red around in his glass, put his nose to the rim sniffing the mellow bouquet and then took a sip of his wine,

'This is a bloody good drop Curly ol' son.'

A Fairly Fiery Dinner Party

Well I've gotta hand it to ya Curly ... that dinner party stunt ya just pulled ... beats anythin' I've ever seen. Y' promised Shaz 'n meself a bit of excitement, and once Curly O'Callahan makes a promise, y' never go back on ya word mate.

These thoughts were ringing in Curly's ears as he climbed into bed that night following Smudge's Birthday celebrations. And when he thought back over the events of the evening, he realised how fortunate both he and Shakes were to have escaped so lightly.

It had all begun shortly after Smudge asked for a second helping of Coq au Vin –

'Any leftovers there Curly? I reckon I could go another serve of that French chook. You've really outdone y'self this time brother.'

'So do y' reckon it's better than a Sund'y roast then Smudge?'

'Well ... that might be stretchin' the friendship a bit Curly. But as you well know, a young tender leg o' spring lamb, accompanied with crisp baked potatas, cauliflour n' white sauce takes a fair bit o' tossin'. On the other hand, I'd have t' agree that this 'ere Cockie Vin has really hit the right spot and is currently runnin' a pretty close second.'

Curly dished up a couple more generous spoonfuls of the rich juicy casserole onto Smudges empty plate.

'Y' betta leave enough room f' dessert though mate, as I'm plannin' to whip up a bit of a specialty of the house.'

'No worries Curl! Takes a lot t' fill a bloke like me up I reckon.'

Curly cleared a space at one end of the table and placed the heavy cast iron pan on top of the copper stand. He then poured methylated spirits into the small container and ignited the burner. But after one too many drinks, Curly was becoming a bit careless, and failed to notice that he'd spilt some of the fluid onto the surface of the tray.

'What's all this caper then Curly ... are you feelin' okay?'

'Yeah ... never better Smudge. I'm plannin' to cook ya up some o' them Crepes Suzettes. I've been practisin' for weeks.'

'Y' sure y're not a bit molly the monk to be attemptin' all this fancy table top cookin'? Them French Mate-a-Dees 'ave to train f' years before they let 'em loose on the customers with all that flambayin' apparatus. I reckon they're a bit like the artisans of the waiterin' industry.'

'What a lot of nonsense Smudge. Curly knows what he's doing.

And it's a pity you couldn't take a leaf out of his book and learn to make yourself a bit more useful around the kitchen.'

'Geez give a bloke a break will y' Shaz. Who do ya reckon grills up them chops 'n snags on the barb-be? I don't recall seein you rushin' in oferin' t' help.'

Curly carefully separated the crepes and placed them into the pan. He then doused and folded each one individually in the tangy juices of orange and lemon before drizzling over a few drops of Grand Marnier.

'Just needs a splash of Cognac, and then ... *voila!* I can promise the both o' ya we'll soon be seein' some impressive fireworks arisin' up from outa the pan.'

'Bloody hell ol' son, is it safe to be sittin' here so close to the action? A bloke's already served his time in Vietnam y' know!'

'No worries Smudge. You're really gunna be amazed when y' experience the end result.'

'Well I'd also like to remind ya Curly, I've grown rather partial to me eyebrows over the years and wouldn't appreciate one o' them extra wide parts runnin' down the cent-a o' me 'ead either mate.'

As Smudge looked on a little anxiously, Curly added the Cognac in readiness to gently flambé the contents, as he'd done so successfully on several previous occasions. Striking the match, he placed the small blue tip to the rim of the pan.

There was a sudden bright flash and the liquid instantly flared.

A huge flame leapt up from the pan licking dangerously close to the curtains and ceiling.

'Gee eez Curly ... are ya sure it's s'posed to be that ...'

Within seconds the fire was showing dangerous signs of billowing out of control; threatening to engulf the entire table.

'Gee eee eez Curly ...'

Curly quickly snatched up the red-hot tray in his bare hands and made a dash for the kitchen sink. Unable to keep it within his grasp, everything toppled onto the floor. The leg of his trousers caught fire and a rivulet of the burning liquid ran across the room in the direction of Shakespeare who had been sleeping quietly in the corner. His tail was now alight, and adding to the chaos, Shakespeare howled along in unison with the ear piercing pitch of the smoke alarm.

Smudge and Shaz were instantly on their feet, scrambling around in circles, grabbing a throw rug from the couch in an attempt to smother the flames and swiftly rescue the victims. The fire shrivelling up Curly's pants was contained as quickly as it had started, and Shaz proved more than capable in a crisis as she set about snuffing out Shakespeare's tail with the aid of several tea towels.

'Phew, that was a really close shave. Are you alright mate? I could picture the whole place goin' up in smoke there f' a few minutes. Me eyebrows bein' only of a secondary concern under these quite unexpected and somewhat surprisin' circumstances!'

'I'm okay, Smudge!'

'And what about poor Shakes?'

Shakespeare appeared unaware as to the exact reason why his sleep had been so rudely interrupted, and even less concerned that his tail had come under the threat of any real danger. Resuming his former position, he plopped back down with a heavy sigh into the corner of the kitchen.

With the acrid smell of smoke and singed dog hair in their nostrils the guests returned to the table.

'Well I've gotta hand it to ya Curly ... that dinner party stunt ya just pulled ... beats anythin' I've ever seen. Y' promised Shaz `n meself a bit of excitement and once Curly O'Callahan makes a promise, y' never go back on ya word mate. I don't expect the ol' ticka could stand up to seein' Shaz pole dancin' though after that outstandin' performance.'

'Well, ya gotta give a bloke full marks for tryin' Smudge!'

Whilst still wearing his smouldering pants, which now appeared a good few inches shorter, Curly retrieved his equipment and began again. Even Shaz was understandably a bit jittery when he struck the match on this second occasion. But to everyone's relief, the sizzling blue flames spread across the pan in a far more confined and orderly manner. And finally they each tucked into their long awaited and extremely delicious dessert. Smudge and Shaz were impressed.

'Blimey these bloody crepes are the best thing I've ever eat'n in me entire life Curly. Bugger the roast mate! I can understand why they've been well worth losin' ya best pair of strides over ol' son, and I think it would be a fittin' and proper moment f' me t' congratulate ya f' providin' a bloke with the most memorable Birthday of a lifetime. Let's hear three cheers f' Curly. Whadda ya reckon there luv!'

A Load Of Rubbish

Shakespeare rushed to the window growling, and stuck his nose between the curtains.

Curly O'Callahan rolled over restlessly, tossing and turning – his sleep disturbed by the sound of clinking bottles. Checking the time on the clock radio, he jumped up out of bed.

'Three-o-three am! What in the blazes is that racket Shakes? Sounds like someone's up to no good in our backyard.'

Shakespeare ran to the door barking and clawing desperately to be released out into the night. Curly unlatched the bolts, switched on the porch light, grabbed a torch and armed himself with his autographed Bradman cricket bat.

Anxious to seek out the intruder, Shakes raced outside in excitement. Curly swung the flashlight around in all directions and noticed that the lid was hanging open on the recycling bin.

'Let's go inside Shakes ... it's freezing out here. Whoever it was, has obviously flown the coop.'

The following morning Curly slipped out to check the bins and just as he'd expected, some cheeky bugger had filled them up to the brim again, leaving no room for his own rubbish. It was that old codger, Charlie Coglan who lived down the road, he would be prepared to bet money on it. Curly felt certain that "Cogs" had a few screws loose lately, especially given the way that he was letting the trash pile up in his garden. Well if he thought that a bloke would be content to just sit back and allow him to get away with this, then he was sadly mistaken. Curly's bins were no convenient receptacle for every Tom, Dick and "Charlie" to rid themselves of their excess garbage.

Everyone in the neighbourhood recognised the fact that Charlie Coglan had become a bit of a hoarder since retiring from his job a couple of years ago. Always cruising the streets in his ute on the lookout for discarded junk tossed out on the nature strips. As luck happened he was out in the garden pulling around some wobbly furniture he'd only recently acquired, when Curly walked up the path to confront him.

'G'day Curly! How's it goin' mate?'

'Well you've got more front than Myers askin' a bloke a question like that Charlie Coglan.'

'What's that s'posed to mean?' Charlie enquired.

'It's me rubbish bins, that I've come to talk about. Seems they're always full. Now why do y' reckon that is?'

'Maybe you should consida givin' away the grog mate.' Charlie replied.

However, when old Charlie Coglan saw the serious expression on Curly's face, he realised that this was no joking matter, and his mood then changed considerably. He was a formidable bloke that didn't take too kindly to criticism. So he stepped up squarely to his neighbour and stared him straight in the eye, then exhaled his stale breath right into Curly's face.

'You accusin' me of a crime or somethin' O'Callahan?'

'I'm accusin' you of no such thing Charlie, 'cept sneakin' around like a thief in the night and off-loadin' ya garbage int' all the neighbourhood bins. Preferably me own, if you want to be a bit more specific about it. And I ask ya, what sort of an inconsiderate *low life* would get up to a cheap trick like that?'

'Well, seems you're not just content with accusin' me of a crime, but also callin' me names on top of all ya other unfounded accusations. And how may I ask did an educated fella such as y'self come to reach this conclusion?'

'It doesn't take too much figurin' out Charlie, after seein' the mess you've got stacked up here in ya front garden.'

'To tell ya the truth O'Callahan, it's really none of your interferin' business what I might choose to do in me own front garden. And I'm sorry to disappoint ya, but you may have t' eat your words before y' grow much older 'cause, one way or another, you're gunna owe me an apology.'

'Oh yeah ... and why's that Charlie?'

'Because I've seen the person responsible for fillin' up the bins with me own two eyes. And a very sad ol' sight it is too I might add. I think that you'll prob'ly be the first to agree when prepared to do a bit more research int' establishin' the correct identity as to the actual perpetrator of this criminal act. Get y' facts straight before runnin' off at the mouth without any proper proof, or I'm tellin' ya – you're gunna come out of this with egg all over ya ugly gob O'Callahan!'

Whilst the bickering between Curly and Charlie was growing increasingly heated, a couple of streets away, Nellie Smithers had awoken to a persistent scuffling inside the cavity of the walls surrounding her bedroom. She stretched her aching limbs beneath the grubby doona, then banged her fist several times against the thin wall in anger.

'Those damned rats are determined to chew their way right through the plaster,' she muttered.

'Grace, I'm awake ... come and help me dress ... Graaace!'

Nellie waited patiently listening for a response. She stuck the tip of her cold red nose further under the bedclothes and mumbled,

'Damn! I don't know what's happened to Grace lately ... she's never around when I need her.'

Apart from occasional scurrying of a mouse along the hollow floorboards, the rats had fled and the house now seemed completely silent. Nellie eased her body into a sitting position, then carefully dangled her thick stumpy legs over the side of the bed. She noticed her clothes piled in a heap on the floor exactly where she had last stepped out of them.

'Looks like Grace forgot to fold me things up again,' she grumbled.

Stooping down rather gingerly, Nellie managed to bundle everything up into her arms.

'Brr ... rr, it's so cold this morning.'

Shivering violently, she fumbled amongst the clothing in search of a t-shirt and clumsily pulled it over the top of her pyjamas. Unaware that the shirt was back to front and inside out Nellie tugged at it in irritation, and then slid each arm into the sleeves of a tattered mohair cardigan. She threw a thick knitted scarf around her neck and placed a Collingwood beanie on top of her uncombed wispy hair. Several failed attempts to push her legs inside a shapeless pair of tracksuit pants finally succeeded and when her icy feet were housed in footy socks and slippers she slowly made her way to the dressing table and dabbed her cheeks with loose white powder and a smudge of bright red rouge.

Nellie inspected herself in the dusty mirror and then applied a crooked line of lip-gloss across her cracked dry mouth. She pressed her lips together firmly then shuffled out slowly through the bedroom door and along the dark drafty passageway. Damp newspapers, books and magazines were strewn along the floor and stacked up everywhere against the walls. When she reached the kitchen, it was cluttered with milk cartons, bottles and cans. Dirty dishes were piled up in a sinkful of cold greasy water and cupboard doors stood ajar revealing the meagre contents of the pantry. Leftover food scraps littered the table and bench tops.

'Grace where are you? Why don't you answer me? This place is such a mess and if you won't tidy up, I'll need to take the baby out walkin' again and drop off some more of this rubbish.'

Nellie hobbled to the back verandah and peered inside an old wicker pram. A porcelain doll surrounded by plastic bags silently stared with wide unseeing eyes back up at her. She snatched up a handful of bags, returned to the kitchen and filled each one with remnants gathered from around the room, then heaved them back into the pram.

'Okay Baby, it's time for a walk. I know you're hiding in there, Grace, and I don't consider this game to be at all funny. I'm off now, and when I get back, we'll boil up the kettle and have a cuppa.'

Nellie made her way out the rear gate and down the laneway. Many of the bins had already been emptied, leaving her disappointed at being too late to sift through in search of her favourite magazines. But at least the heavy bundles could be more easily disposed of.

'Think we might take a stroll around the block, now that the sun is shining Baby.'

Nellie innocently continued along the street in the direction of Charlie's house, happy in the knowledge that she'd helped to tidy up the kitchen. Grace would be so proud of her once she grew tired of that silly game.

'Isn't that Nellie Smithers comin' down the street?' Curly asked Charlie.

'Yep ... that's her alright! She's gone a bit funny since 'er sister Grace passed away.'

'What's she doin' pushin' a pram around?' Curly enquired.

'Well, truth is, Nellie's the culprit whose dumpin' the rubbish O'Callahan.'

Curly looked astounded.

'What's the matter Curly – cat got y' tongue all of a sudden?'

'It's just that I can't believe this is really the same sheila. Have a look at the state she's in.' Curly remarked, ignoring Charlie's sarcasm.

'I've already taken the matter in hand, 'n even organised a social worker to come round and see 'er.'

'Well Charlie ... looks like I've made a bit of a blue!'

'Is that all y've got t' say f' y'self O' Callahan? A bit of a bloody blue is it! Just let that be a lesson to ya in the future before ya go rushin' in and makin' rash judgments.'

Curly placed a hand up to his bright red face to make certain that he didn't have egg all over his ugly gob as Charlie had just moments earlier so positively predicted.

'Y' know Charlie ... I suspect Nellie was in me backyard in the early hours of the mornin' probably dressed in those thin damp rags and slippers she's now wearin'. It's a wonder she's still alive poor devil.'

A Load Of Rubbish

Nellie wheeled the pram up to Charlie's front fence.

'Good mornin' Nellie.'

'Hello Mr. Coglan.'

'What are you doin' shufflin' around the street in them thin slippers?'

'Aw ... forgot to put me boots on. Grace is home hidin' and I'm not sure what to do without 'er tellin' me 'xactly what she expec's. I had t' walk the baby ya see.'

'Well why don't you come inside and have a cup of tea ... warm y'self up a bit by the fire?'

'Nup ... gotta get back home and put the baby to bed. Grace will be worryin'.'

'Well I'm not sure if you remember, but this 'ere's Curly O'Callahan from down the road, and he's a bit concerned about ya. Naturally bein' the well mannered 'n kindly gentleman that 'e is,' Charlie paused and looked pointedly at Curly, 'he's offered to see ya safely to ya doorstep.'

Nellie seemed happy to walk the short distance back home with Curly, and when they reached the gate she was greeted by some new friends who had come to call on her with warm clothes, soup and her favourite magazines. "Oh goodie" she thought "Now they can help me to find Grace."

Later that night as Curly O'Callahan settled back into bed he let out a deep sigh.

'Well Shakes, looks like I made a bit of a dill of meself t'day accusin' old Cogs of fillin' up the wheelie bins.'

Shakespeare padded to the side of the bed and placed his paw on Curly's arm.

'S'pose a bloke's allowed t' make an honest mistake every now 'n again, or he woudn't be human. But f' the life o' me Shakes, I just couldn't bring meself t' apologise properly t' ol' Charlie while 'e was wearin' that smug look all over his whiskery dial. Anyhow, at least I can hope poor Nellie Smithers is sleepin' safely in a clean dry bed t'night with a warm healthy meal inside 'er. I worry about what tomorra might bring though Shakes. Still ... reckon worryin's not gunna do anyone much good, so maybe we should try and get a bit o' shut eye now fella, and I'm sure everything'll look a whole lot brighter in the mornin.'

Curly reached out and switched off the light. Then pulling the blankets up around his chin, he yawned loudly and rolled over. 'Night Shakes!' It took some time for him to finally doze off, and just as he started to fall into a really deep sleep, all of a sudden his eyes flicked wide open. There was a distinct feeling of déjà vu as Shakespeare rushed to the window growling and stuck his nose between the curtains.

Curly heard a familiar noise. Clink ... clink ... clink.

What's Love Got T' Do With It?

'Haven't heard much about y' writin' class of late Curly!'

'I reckon we're gunna be tacklin' the subject of *love* this term Smudge.'

'Gawd stone the flamin' crows, this must be y' lucky year ol' son. You should be a bloody expert in the field, given your broad knowledge 'n experience with the sheilas.'

'Aw ... come off it Smudge. Anyone'd think I'm some sort of a philanderin' sex maniac the way you make a bloke out t' sound. There's more t' the words *love* 'n romance than just jumpin' int' bed ya know.'

'Well I'm not completely lackin' in feelin's ol' son. After all me 'n the missus have been shacked up f' quite a numba o' years if y' do recall. An' considerin' you were me best man 'n all, it would be decent of ya t' give a certain degree of recognition n' respect t' the fact.'

'I haven't forgotten Smudge, and that's why I was wonderin'

how you'd feel about helpin' a bloke out and lettin' me run a coupla quick questions past ya?'

'What about mate?'

'About ... well ... y' know ... *love*, o' course!'

'Reckon that'd be sort o' me own private business there, Curly. Y' don't think Shaz 'd appreciate me speakin' outa school n' sharin' our innermost emotions that we vowed t' keep sacred between just the two of us.'

'Geez don't go gettin' on y' high horse there, Smudge ... a bloke's not talkin' here about what tricks y' get up to. I'm interested in what y' thoughts concernin' *love* might be in more general and meanin'ful terms.'

'Keep y'self nice there Curly ol' son. Me fantasies are just as much me own private business as what me marriage is.'

'Fair dinkum Smudge, I s'pose *love's* not the sort o' thing blokes discuss down the pub. But we've been mates for a long time, and I don't remember y' ever bein' so coy or unwillin' t' share ya secrets with me in the past.'

'Well if Shaz ever got wind of even a quarta of the stuff a bloke got up to in amongst sowin' his wild oats, that'd be it mate. Curtains f' ol' Smudge 'ere. I'd 'ave me bloody throat cut. Not t' mention nuthin' about what might happen t' another more relevant area of me fragile anatomy. An' that's not necessarily guaranteed t' occur in exactly that order either mate.'

'Strewth that's takin' things a bit t' the extreme isn't it Smudge?

Surely Shaz is not gunna be that upset about y' havin' a small informal chat about the matter.'

'Believe me ol' son, once y' get roped int' actually tyin' the knot, a sheila can turn on a bloke as quick as winkin'. There's no such words as small or informal in a woman's vocabulary when she gets crooked on ya about somethin'. An' at the risk of losin' me ol' fella, I can't impress on ya too strongly Curly, the thought of reflectin' upon this age-old subject couldn't possibly get any deeper or more sensitive. A bloke's life just wouldn't be worth livin'. It's as simple as that. There'd be nothin' more painful than f' me to admit t' anythin' even remotely revealin' regardin' this topic.'

'What about romance then, Smudge?'

'Gawd blimey, y' drive a hard bargain Curly O'Callahan, I'll say that f' ya. Never give up ... do ya! If it's romance ya really wanna talk about, as you well know, I don't try 'n hide the fact that I've done me fair share of wooin' the sheilas. Plyin' 'em with flowers 'n chocies. Tellin' 'em how good they look. But o' course, you 'n I are both aware of the biggest cardinal sin.'

'What's that Smudge?'

'Neva let 'em catch ya checkin' out the competition. An' that's a tough call with all them good sorts walkin' around. Always hang back a little to the rear if ya get me drift there Curly. A bit like the Queen n' the Duke mate. 'E's not as silly as 'e looks that bloke ya know!'

'So then Smudge, what would ya consider t' be one of the

most memorable love scenes y've ever seen at the pitchas f' instance?'

'That's easy ol' son. It was *William Holden* dancin' t' *Moonglow* with *Kim Novak* in a movie called *Picnic*. That steamy moment has stayed in me mind f'rever. Kim Novak had all 'er clothes on at the time Curly ... but them two dancin' was charged with steamy electrical currents that was more touchin' than anythin' I've ever seen before or since.'

'But Smudge, a lot of me friends at the writin' group are too young to remember *William Holden*. Do ya reckon there's anyone that currently runs a close second?'

'Shaz'd prob'ly say *Richard Gere*. She fancied him in another pitcha about dancin' as well.

He was secretly attendin' ballroom dancin' classes 'n havin' 'imself a few lessons under the tutelage of *Jennifer Lopez*. As ya can well appreciate Curly this was a great sacrifice on 'is part havin' t' keep all this knowledge under 'is hat so t' speak. But when his missus *Susan Sarandan* discovered what he was doin', she went along to see 'im in a competition thinkin' that 'e had the hots for some other sheila. Believe me Curly when he's prepared t' chuck in the dancin' n' comes up that escalator in his white tuxedo carryin' a red rose for his missus, Shaz was cryin' tears of joy. Now that was what y'd call a true 'n proper example of *love* mate.'

'So t' get back t' me original question then. How do ya really reckon a bloke knows he's in *love*?'

'Y're a persistent ol' bugger Curly. This is all a bit too profound f' the likes o' someone such as meself ya understand, so I'm plannin' on cheatin' here a bit an' lookin' up me Thesaurus.'

'Geez, since when did you come to own a Thesaurus Smudge?'

'I'll let that one go through t' the keeper ol' son and sum this whole argument up in one short sentence. Now let's see ... here we are, *Love – A score o' zero (in tennis, squash etc.)*. Guess we might have t' scrap that one off the list in this particular instance. *Love – A very strong feelin' of affection.* I'm getting' hot here mate. *Love – A strong feelin' of affection linked with sexual attraction.* Right on the button. Satisfied now – Curly me ol' mate?'

Curly's Lost Love

Don't step on a crack or you'll break your mother's back!

Curly was out walking Shakespeare ... his eyes cast down towards the uneven footpath as he tread carefully, at times a little anxious about tripping over.

Don't step on a crack or you'll break your mother's back!

It was Geri's voice he could hear inside his head. She used to repeat that rhyme to him when they were kids. But at this late stage of his life, with his mum no longer having any need to worry, maybe Geraldine was slightly more concerned about reminding Curly to protect his own aging bones. Yet the idea of a grown man even contemplating the thought of trying to avoid cracks seemed really quite foolish.

Curly tugged back gently on Shakespeare's leash.

'Let's hope a bloke's not becoming senile now I've reached me senior years Shakes. P'rhaps we should ease up on the pace a bit!'

Geraldine Delaney had once been the love of Curly's life. He could still see her quite clearly skipping down the pathway up ahead as though it were yesterday. It must have been a challenge to skip and avoid landing on a crack. He'd never really given it much thought until recently. But even though Geraldine was younger, he had learnt to take heed of her advice. They'd grown up together and lived in the same street. Curly had been best mates with her older brother.

He chuckled to himself as he remembered a shy little girl with straight brown hair and freckles dotted across the bridge of her nose. She was always trailing around behind the two of them wanting to join in.

'Can I come 'n play with yous' two?' she persisted.

'Get lost Geri! Go 'n play dolls with the girls!' her brother shouted. And boys, being boys, had thought it natural to shun her, and run away. Both in full agreement that the last thing they needed was a nuisance kid hanging around messing up their plans.

'Wait! Wait for me!' she pleaded.

Curly had felt guilty whenever he looked back over his shoulder and saw the tears of rejection spring into her eyes. But there were of course times when they did reluctantly permit her to string along. Yet even at that stage, in the innocence of his youth, he had always been aware that there was something he especially liked about his friend's younger sister.

'Ya know what Shakes? I've never told a single soul about how much I loved Geraldine Delaney. She broke me heart. But it wasn't her fault ya know. Unfortunately, from me own point o' view, she just never seemed t' come t' terms with the fact that I wasn't really her brother.'

As Curly grew into his teenage years, things began to change. Both he and Geri started moving in the same circles and developed an interest in learning to dance. Geri now wore her once short hair in a cute ponytail and Curly slowly began to notice that he was forming a strong attachment to her. An unspoken bond was to then quickly blossom into a mutually close friendship. Curly came to realise that this little girl from down the street whom he had once been so intent on running away from, was fast proving to be the young woman that he might well wish to marry.

However, Curly's dream appeared to be a little one sided, as Geraldine didn't seem aware of his emotional commitment and failed to share in his passionate feelings. She'd always looked upon Curly as a brother and had never considered the possibility of establishing any sort of romantic relationship with him.

For years Curly suffered with a broken heart as he stood back on the sidelines watching each new boyfriend that Geraldine welcomed into her life. He journeyed to England. They constantly exchanged letters, and in his absence he held out the hope that Geraldine might come to think of him in a different light.

Curly returned with renewed optimism believing that their friendship may have developed into something more serious. In disappointment, he discovered that Geri had a new man in her life. Their relationship was destined to remain unchanged.

Yet patiently he waited, expecting that one day she might look at him in the same way as he had seen her look upon many of her other more fortunate suitors. But fearing rejection, not once did he ever reveal how much he loved her.

Geraldine Delaney eventually married another, and remained friends with Curly throughout her entire lifetime without ever learning the truth.

'I often wondered if she'd guessed. What do ya reckon Shakes?' With sad eyes, Shakespeare looked up at Curly and gave him a sympathetic woof.

Many years later Geraldine became ill, and following her death, Curly spoke at the funeral telling the mourners that he had always loved her. But when he looked down into the front row to glimpse the grieving faces of her husband and children, he concluded,

'Geri was like a sister to me!'

His secret has remained undisclosed until this very day. And now, out of respect for this little girl he had loved, Curly avoided the cracks in the footpath.

'Remember now Shakes ... don't go steppin' on them cracks!' he warned. `Geri is watchin'!'

As Curly continued his walk he looked ahead up the pathway.

'Wait, wait for me!' he tearfully pleaded. But sadly Geraldine Delaney slowly turned away and faded from view.

'Please come back Geri, I've got something to tell you!'

Nothin's Happenin'

'Gee Shakes ... I hate t' say it ... but I reckon a bloke's sufferin' from writers' block. Happens to all them great authors y' understand! That's why so many take themselves off to a turret in France, where they can concentrate on their work without bein' interrupted.

I can recall a well known sheila who, at the age of fifty, reached one o' them mid-life crisis situations. Well she wouldn't be on 'er Pat Malone now would she mate? Anyhow, p'rhaps well recognisin' the fact, and thinkin' there could be a bob or two to be made in the process ... what d' y' reckon she did?'

Shakespeare let out a slight whimper in polite response, but was really wondering when Curly might remember to fill up his empty bowl with Goodoos.

'Just up 'n packed 'er bags, left her family and jetted off t' the other side of the world f' a year or two, where she lobbed at some romantic French village. Armed with 'er writin' tools, she threw the shutters open and placed her notepad down on a desktop in some sun drenched room. The view from the casement window spillin' over with bright red geraniums, looked out beyond the cobbled laneways to the distant fields of lavender. That's the all important ingredient for success Shakes, t' be able to see the lavender. Any artist'll tell y' that. Her plan was t' sample a whole lot o' high livin', which included winin', dinin' an' cavortin', providin' her with just enough senseless drivel to stick int' a book. And accordin' to all accounts, she'd 'av ya believin' them French gigolos were just waitin' in line t' seduce her.

But doesn't really matter what a bloke such as meself might think about her source of inspiration – y' can't dispute the fact that she was an enta-prizin' writer Shakes! Prob'ly made a tidy sum sellin' 'er fairytale t' every tired and disgruntled fifty year old housewife around the country mate.

Well I can promise ya I'd never go off and leave you behind fella, no matter how desperate a bloke is to produce a story! If I can't write here on me own home turf alongside me best mate, much an' all as I love the French countryside, there's nowhere else on earth I'd wanna write.'

Shakespeare lifted his chin from his paws and leant his head slightly to one side, trying to figure out why Curly was on the one hand so worked up, and yet still seemed fairly pleased with himself.

'But there's a lesson to be learnt from this little tale I reckon. It's important to keep writin' even if nothin's happenin'. O' course this could be a bit disappointin' for the reader whose expectin' to hear a stimulatin' plot if y' follow me meanin'. That's the time when a vivid imagination can really come int' play! Yet all them experts seem t' agree, if y' wanna produce a bestseller, it's essential t' plant y' bum firmly on the seat and keep pluggin' away at the keyboard every single day. I'll let y' in on a secret though Shakes, writin' just doesn't happen. In me own case, somethin' magical makes it happen. Somethin' ya gotta believe in with y' whole heart 'n soul. It's a bit like any worthwhile passion in life.

Can't y' just hear ol' Smudge philosophisin' from afar. Y' know what the problem is, don't cha ol' son? It's lack of exercise. Well maybe he's right. We haven't been for a walk today, what with the rain 'n all. It's not too invitin' outside, but p'rhaps I'll get me top on and we'll head off around the block. Maybe this'll give me brain a chance t' re-energize. But y' do realise, most would agree, it can't be compared t' wanderin' the cobble stoned laneways somewhere in Provence. That's in France y' know Shakes.'

At the mention of the word walk, Shakespeare leapt up in excitement. He really couldn't give a flying plastic schmacko about the fact that he wouldn't be stepping one paw outside the immediate vicinity of the all too familiar streets around the local neighbourhood. Any sort of a walk was a good walk. He didn't need to be shipped across to Provence to enjoy himself.

After their return, Curly asked, 'Well Shakes, how d' y' feel now since our little outin'? What did you observe along the way?'

Shakespeare yawned and flopped down in front of the heater. He thought to himself, those couple of trees in the nature strip around the corner were a great place to take a leak. And he was fond of the Andersons' end post along their picket fence where the small patch of weeds smelt particularly interesting and juicy.

'Never am all that eager to get out 'n exercise though mate. But once we hit that front gate, there is a feelin' of exhilaration when the breeze touches y' face and the gentle sunlight peeks through them clouds. Although at times walkin' in the same direction can become a bit tiresome. But then y' think how great it is t' have the freedom t' get out 'n about. Nothin' is to be taken f' granted in this life y' realise Shakes. Yet I'd have t' admit, with the absence of anythin' even remotely inspirin' t' prod me thoughts, I guess maybe we'll just have t' call it a day and come back 'n try again t'morrow.'

Shakespeare curled up into a tight ball and sighed. He wasn't sure why Curly worried so much about his writing. A dog's life was a whole lot less complicated and pretty good as far as he was concerned.

A Stressful Assignment

'How's ya writin' class comin' along now Curly?'

'Aw ... it's okay Smudge.'

'Y' don't sound too convincin' mate. Struck some sort of a snag have ya?'

'Nup, not exactly.'

'Was there a problem with ya love story?'

'Nup.'

'Well this isn't like you. What's with the sudden lack of enthusiasm?'

Curly seemed unusually quiet and made a point of studying some obscure spot on the ceiling. Smudge quickly followed suit, wondering just what the hell was so interesting up above their heads.

'Every time a bloke get's the roof freshly painted, them bloody possums keep leakin' all over the ceilin'!'

'With all due respect Curly, f' a minute there I thought someone musta stolen the last two cans outa the fridge mate.'

'It's no jokin' matter Smudge. Them possums keep a bloke awake half the night. One even fell down me chimney last week and Shakes 'n meself was chasin' it all round the house.

'Geez ya shoulda sung out ol' son 'n I coulda come over with me shot gun. That woulda sorted the bugger out in a 'urry.'

'That's illegal Smudge. Possums are a protected species y' know. Besides, you're not s'posed to be in possession of one o' them firearms without a proper licence.'

'Dunno what's up with ya lately Curly. I'm only pullin' y' leg o' course. But judgin' by that big frown y're wearin', I can't 'elp gettin' the distinct impression that there's more on ya mind than possums.'

'Well if y' really wanna know, it's Penelope. You remember me mentionin' her don't ya Smudge?'

'Penny-lope! Geez a bloke could hardly forget a name like that in a hurry. Don't tell me she's after ya ol' son?'

'Bloody hell Smudge. Knock it off will ya.'

'Sorry Curly. Didn't mean t' go upsettin' ya. Why what's been happenin' mate?'

'Well y' see, we've got this bit of an assignment comin' up, and Penelope Winters pulled me name out o' the hat. She's gotta interview me about me writin'.'

'An' what's wrong with that Curly?'

'I don't really know 'er, and she asked me to meet 'er for a coffee at the Shoppin' Plaza.'

'I reckon that seems pretty straight forward.'

'Smudge I was wonderin' if you weren't too busy ...'

'Hey hang on a minute Curly. Forget about ropin' me int' this one. Shootin' a possum is one thing but a bloke draws the line at riskin' me reputation. Wouldn't fancy 'er jumpin' t' any wrong conclusions.'

'F' God's sake Smudge, ya don't actually believe she's gunna think we're ...'

'Well y' can't be too careful, that's all I'm sayin' Curly. Any'ow, what's so scary about bein' with a woman? It's not as though the two o' yas are gunna be on ya Pat Malone, what with bein' surrounded by all them noisy shoppers.'

'But I don't really know 'er Smudge.'

'Yeah, I think we've already established that mate.'

'Maybe you could bring Shaz with ya?'

'An' how in the hell are y' gunna go about explainin' the two of us taggin' along?'

'It's kinda hard t' get me head around. Y' see, there's somethin' about 'er that completely unnerves me. It's like I get tongue tied and can't express meself properly.'

'Since when 'ave you ever had a problem chattin' up the sheilas? Sounds t' me like you've taken a bit o' a shine to 'er, brother!'

'Strewth, I wouldn't o' thought so mate! She's not my type at all.'

'Then how can y' account f' this strange phenomenon that's takin' place inside ya?'

'She strikes me as bein' just a bit too proper or somethin', 'n I feel like I've gotta watch me p's 'n q's.'

'Seems to me like ya gotta watch more than ya bloody p's 'n q's Curly. A bit of a prima donna by the sound of 'er. Them sheilas are high maintenance I reckon. If ya want my advice Curl, give 'er the flick pass mate.'

'Hey, hang on Smudge ... I'm not plannin' on askin' 'er to marry me. It's just coffee and 'n interview we're talkin' here.'

'Don't let 'em fool ya ol' son. How can ya be certain that this hat pullin' caper wasn't rigged?'

'Geez ... y' can't be serious! We weren't holdin' a union ballot here Smudge. This is me writin' class we're talkin' about. I'm strugglin' with the whole idea as it is, and was countin' on you bein' me best mate 'n all, to give a bloke some sort of positive feedback 'n a bit of a friendly chop out.'

'Well Curly, I've told ya before how I feel. She's just not right f' ya, and the mere fact that Penny-lope drew your name outa that hat, seems kinda suspicious like t' me. So I think y' should simply give 'er a call and tell 'er you've come down with some sorta highly contagious bug or somethin'.'

'I can't do that. She'd know I was lyin' as soon as she hears me voice.'

'Put one of them hankies over the mouthpiece.'

'Nup ... just wouldn't seem right some'ow. I can't see any way out of it. I've gotta go along and get this thing off me plate. Then it'll be over and done with f' good.'

'If ya so dead set on meetin' up with 'er, and wanna settle ya nerves ... my advice would be to down a couple o' quick sherbets before ya 'ead off.'

'I don't wanna be smellin' like a boozer first thing in the mornin' Smudge.'

'Just whack on a some o' that "You go Boss" aftershave Shaz bought ya last Christmas. Then squirt a bit o' that breath freshener int' ya gob Curly and you'll come up smellin' sweeter than a rose.'

'Do ya really think that's me best option then Smudge?'

'No worries mate. You'll be so calm you'll 'ave 'er eatin outa ya hands before ya even take ya first mouthful o' coffee. But rest assured, to me own way o' thinkin', as I've told ya before, ya need to get y'self an uncomplicated sort o' va sheila whose not gunna be raisin' too many issues. At this point in a bloke's life Curly ol' son, ya just wanna keep it simple ... avoidin' any unnecessary complications and puttin' extra stress onta the ol` ticka, 'n more importantly, the ol' hip pocket.'

'It's only a cup of coffee Smudge. Don't think that'll break the bank.'

'Well depends what time ya meetin' 'er. Ya could be up f' one o' them fancy I-talian foccacias 'n then she'll be hangin' out f' a lemon curd tart. Next thing ya know there'll be a need f' another cappucino. It all mounts up and eats int' the monetary resources if y' get me drift.'

'But ya don't really think she'll be expectin' a bloke to buy 'er lunch, do ya? It's not as though I asked her out on a date. She's invitin' me f' coffee remember.'

'I'll make ya a little wager Curly. After y've settled y'self at the cafe, she'll leave ya sittin' there, hangin' around like a shag on a rock waitin'. An' when she finally decides t' arrive all flustered 'n apologetic, guess who'll be doin' the shoutin' while she's busy rootin' around in 'er handbag.'

'Well Smudge, I'm tellin' ya right now ... I can stretch the budget to a coupla cappucinos and even a a slice o' toasted raisin bread. But no matter what ya might reckon, there's absolutely no chance of a bloke such as m'self ever teamin' up with a sheila like Penelope Winters.'

'Curly, it wouldn't be the first time an unsuspectin' fella just goin' about his normal day to day business has been sucked in by a cunnin' sheila. Maybe there ain't too many of 'em called Penny-lope mind ja. So just remember t' heed me warnin' 'n hang back when it comes t' bein' overly polite 'n obligin'. An' don't go tellin' 'er any of ya private business. Just stick t' the subject of writin'. A simple yes 'n no will suffice! I wish ya the best o' luck ol' son ... n' at this crucial stage o' the predicament, that's about the most favourable advice a mate can offer ya!'

The Interview

As Curly prepared himself for his meeting with Penelope, he decided to take Smudge's advice and indulge in a couple of quick whiskies to settle his nerves.

'Well Shakes ... wish me luck. I'll be on me way now, and by the time I get back, a bloke'll be lookin' to pull the top off a nice cold can. Reckon I might have earnt a beer by then. It's been quite a while since I've had coffee with a sheila, an' as y' might well understand, I don't wanna go makin' a complete galah of meself. So as I'm a bit outa practise, don't go forgettin' t' just keep them paws crossed ol' pal.'

Shakespeare crossed his legs and looked up affectionately into Curly's eyes.

Curly was feeling fairly neat and dapper as he caught a glimpse of himself in the mirror on the way through from the car park. *Geez is that really me? A bloke doesn't come up too badly with a bit of the ol' spit 'n polish,* he thought approvingly. Suddenly he felt a warm inner glow. Smudge had been right as usual. The whisky was working and Curly became aware of a renewed surge of confidence.

The glass door smoothly slid open and in the distance he immediately spotted Penelope already seated at the coffee lounge located right in line with the entrance. *How in the hell did that happen? Accordin' t' Smudge's calculations, Penelope wasn't s'posed to arrive ahead of him.* He quickly ducked behind a post – his confidence now being tested. He needed to calmly collect his thoughts. *This had really thrown a spanner into the works, as he'd been plannin' all along t' be here first.* Peeping around the edge of the pillar, he momentarily observed her, spying before she had a chance to see him. Her head was lowered and she appeared to be reading the menu. *Well y' can't stand here hidin' all day Curly O'Callahan, it's time to get on with it.*

As he stepped out into the open and slowly approached the table, she looked up and removing her glasses rather formally reached out her hand and greeted him with a broad friendly smile. *Not a bad lookin' sheila for her age all things bein' equalled. An' I'm gettin' a funny feelin' she kinda likes me.* Curly thought with satisfaction.

'How are you Curly? I'm so glad that you could come.'

'Well, yeah ... I'm okay P ... Penelope. Hope I haven't kept y' waitin'?'

'No ... you're right on the dot in fact. I was a few minutes early. But before we get started, I've been meaning to say to you, please call me Penny if you'd prefer. Most of my friends find it easier.'

Gee that oughta shut Smudge up for a while. Even the boys at the Pub shouldn't have a problem copin' with a name as simple as 'Penny'.

'Aah ... could I getcha a coffee then Penny?'

'That's very nice of you thanks Curly, but I've already ordered. Hope a cappuccino will be okay ... I wasn't sure what you preferred!'

'Yeah, that's fine with me.' Curly replied, reaching inside a pocket for his wallet.

'Please don't worry ... this one's on me Curly.'

Thought Smudge warned me that I'd be doin' all the shoutin'.

When they were both settled, he realised that Penelope Winters seemed a bit ill at ease as she flicked opened the pages of a notepad and now placed it squarely on the tabletop in front of her – hands slightly trembling. *Was it possible that this whole idea was just as unsettling for her as it was for him?*

'Curly, I'm sure you understand that I've never done anything like this before, and am not really certain about the questions that I should be asking.'

Anythin' like what ... before? Curly thought.

'Well as long as y' won't be too shocked t' hear about me jail sentence 'n the time I was locked up with me mentor Choppa Reid. He's a revelation that bloke. Done a bit o' writin' himself ya know!'

Penelope's face went pale and her mouth dropped open. *Bloody hell! He knew he shouldn't have drank that second whisky. Now he was actually attemptin' extremely bad humour. Where did that stupid remark spring from?*

'Sorry Penny, just couldn't help meself there f' a minute. The serious look on y' face sorta cracked me up a bit.'

Curly then kicked himself. *I shouldn't be making comments about her face. Women are extremely sensitive about their looks.*

'Gosh, you really had me going there Curly. For one moment, I actually believed you were serious!'

Following Curly's brave effort to break the ice, they both laughed and suddenly the air was filled with a bit less tension.

'I did see Chopper Reid on *Australian Story* a few months ago promoting his book, and believe me the things I was hearing, would have made your hair curl. Oh ... no offence intended there, Curly.'

'Aw ... that's okay Penny. But yeah ... sharin' a cell with Choppa would be a bit of a day to day proposition I reckon. If he took a sudden dislikin' to the colour of y' toothbrush, you'd be likely to wake up one morning to find y'self dissected into tiny little pieces 'n sprinkled in with his cornflakes. S'pect that'd be the end of a buddin' writin' career!'

'Well it's certainly food for thought!' Penny chuckled. 'But if y' don't mind too much Curly, my first query has nothing to do with the writing or even Chopper Reid for that matter ... it's just basically more about a woman's curiosity really.'

'Well just so long as it's not one of them trick questions!'

'No I don't believe so. I was wondering if you would mind my asking if *Curly* is a nickname?'

'I s'pose most of me mates `d say so! But I reckon I'd be tellin' a fib if I led ya to believe anythin' other than the facts. Y' see, strictly speakin' I was christened *Michael Curlow O'Callahan. Curlow* bein' me mother's maiden name. Think me mum was a bit reluctant to let go of 'er own identity when she married into the O'Callahan family.'

'I can well understand that situation Curly and am in full agreement. Why should we women have to give up our name?'

'Well I think maybe I should steer clear of anythin' bein' of a controversial nature, but t' continue on with the story ... *Michael* was me paternal Grandfather's name, which was sort o' thrust upon me, as opposed to bein' a name of me mum's own choosin'. Tradition ... I s'pose you'd call it!'

'How unfair and totally antiquated is that!'

'Think maybe you and me ol' mum may have had a coupla things in common there Penny. Any'ow, don't believe me mother quite saw eye t' eye with me Grandfather. So as a result of some rift between 'em, I've been answerin' to *Curly* for as long as I can remember. S'pect me best mate Smudge would be a bit surprised if he ever discovered that *Curly* is short f' *Curlow*. A bloke 'd never hear the end of it.'

'But surely your best friend ... ah was that Smudge ... is familiar with your full name Curly?'

The Interview

'I reckon he's never really twigged or put a lot o' thought int' the matter of associatin' *Curly* with me middle name. But don't get me wrong, it's not that I'm not proud of it. Just think the less attention I draw to pointin' certain things out, the better. Smudge'd probably start callin' me *Curlow* just t' rev a bloke up. He's always foolin' around y' understand and testin' the waters.'

'Well I'm probably unlikely to be running into your friend Smudge, so the truth is safe with me Curly.'

'Reckon it's not somethin' that's gunna be keepin' me awake of a night. There's no great secret attached to it or anythin'. At this late stage of a bloke's career I've got more pressin' matters t' worry about rather than thinkin' of changin' me name back t' Michael. All me mates 'd be wonderin' what the hell was goin' on!'

'And what about *Smudge*? Sounds like an interesting character Curly!'

'Well, truth is unless you've got a coupla days to spare, a bloke'd have a bit o' trouble doin' me mate justice in tryin' t' describe his considerable attributes in the space of ten short minutes.'

'So maybe we should move on to the more relevant questions. What got you interested in writing and when did you first get started?'

The interview continued ...

'Thank you Curly. This has been an enjoyable way to get to know you a little better. I hope that from the information compiled,

I can do a worthy job of putting together an interesting article about your particular approach to writing.'

When Curly walked away from the shopping centre he was relieved with how smoothly everything had turned out. *Penelope Winters seemed like a decent enough sort of a sheila.* He was surprised that he'd told her about his name. Yet wondered what harm it could have done. Although he did notice she seemed to have very definite ideas. But that wasn't such a bad thing either!'

Shortly after arriving home he received a call from Smudge.

'Well how did ja get on Curly? Did Penny-lope put the hard word on ya ol' son?'

'Geez Smudge ... there was really nothin' sinister goin' on. But those two whiskies I drank before leavin' home made me a bit careless with some of me conversation. Not sure how she responded to a few of me silly jokes, as she seems a bit on the serious side I reckon.'

'Yeah ... well you mark me words now Curly, it's them innocent ones that ya gotta watch out f'. Keep ya guard up, or next thing y' know, she'll be wantin' ya t' pay a friendly visit t' fix a leaky tap or somethin'. Just watch y'self ol' son.'

'You're over-reactin' Smudge.'

'We'll see mate ... we'll see!'

Geraldine

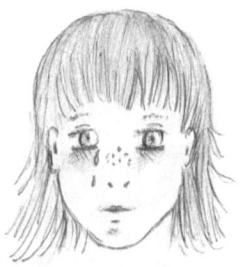

You were there at every turn Curly. At times in the foreground ... at times in the background. But Curly ... you were always there!

'We've already met! Well perhaps not quite in the usual sense, as such a formality is no longer possible. You see, my days on this earth ended several years ago.

My name is Geri ... Geraldine Delaney.

Don't step on a crack or you'll break your mother's back!

Surely now you do remember me. For it was my good friend, Curly O'Callahan, who so recently introduced us, and revealed to you his secret. And in so doing ... I heard his voice call out to me.

I am that little girl responsible for having so innocently broken his heart.

Well Curly, it's for you that I've since felt an urgent need to put pen to paper and in my ghostly hand, inform you of the good news. Sometimes hearts can be mended. And sometimes, good fortune is bound to smile down on you.

It's true that my love for you was never of the romantic kind My childhood adoration was that borne by a little girl.

I struggled to notice at just what stage you grew into a man, but when reaching my early teens, I joined you at ballroom dancing classes. We pedalled our bikes together. We ate hamburgers, drank chocolate milk shakes and laughed together. And later, when you bought your first car, not once did you ever pass by the Delaney home without stopping to collect me.

Dancing continued throughout the following decade and the bond which I had once considered to be nothing more than an innocent brother and sisterly affection, had by this stage developed into a friendship of a far more significant nature. At the time I understood that we shared something special, but I did not think of it as falling in love dear Curly.

It was during these years that I experienced the carefreeness and funfilled days of youth. The days of rock 'n roll and beehives. Of stolen kisses and fogged up windows at the drive-in. Of summer beach parties and holiday romances. The days of Bandstand, the Everley brothers, Bill Hayley and Elvis. You were there at every turn. At times in the foreground ... at times in the background. But Curly ... you were always there!

I did see you Curly, but I was far too busy to notice the sadness in your eyes.

Suddenly, without so much as a moments notice, you left and travelled far away to work in England. I never questioned why you did that Curly. We corresponded regularly - your return almost appearing as unexpected as your leaving. You seemed in high spirits accusing me of sending a mysterious typewritten love letter. You joked about it. But no, it wasn't me! I protested. You seemed reluctant to take my word for it, as though believing I was deliberately teasing you. Maybe convincing yourself that I was too shy to admit my true feelings.

Was there really such a letter, or were you merely testing me? Yet not once did you alert me as to how you really felt or hint of anything remotely romantic between us.

On the occasion of your twenty-first Birthday, Curly you crossed me off your invitation list, leaving your mother to explain the reason why my most special of friends had chosen to exclude me. There was a moment of disbelief followed by a feeling of sadness and disappointment.

Several years later when I married, you met Christine. I was happy, thinking you had at last found someone whom you might be willing to share your life with. However Curly ... you had other plans!

We kept in touch throughout the years and six weeks before my death, you rang me for the last time. We said our hasty goodbyes knowing we would never speak again.

We were mistaken! I heard your voice calling me as recently as last week. Please come back Geri, you said, I've got something to tell you!

No need dear Curly, for I am right beside you. As I look back over my life, how could I have never known? Perhaps I have always known but neglected to acknowledge the truth. Please forgive me if I once broke your heart. I have loved you Curly in a way that exceeds mere romantic infatuation, which in time, so often fades and dies. I have loved you for just being you ... my hero and my lifelong friend!

Take care now Curly, and until we meet again, always remember – Don't step on a crack or you'll break your mother's back!'

A Message From The Other Side

'Smudge ... I've been thinkin' ... do y' reckon it might be possible t' communicate with someone who has ... well y' know ... passed on?'

'Passed on! As in kicked the bloody bucket y' mean mate! Blimey, ya not thinkin' of packin' it in are ya Curly? Surely life's not treatin' ya that badly?'

'It's nothin' like that Smudge. Just wanted t' get ya thoughts about the more spiritual side o' things really.'

'Well let's see now Curly ol' son,' Smudge said scratching his head. `I s'pose a bloke'd have t' say there's nothin' much stoppin' any of 's from strikin' up a bit of a one sided conversation. I've heard of plenty o' people who regularly do just that. But surely ya own common sense'd pretty soon tell ya, that y' wouldn't wanna be left hangin' by the short 'n curlies while waitin' fer a bloody answer now would ya mate? Why? Are y' plannin' on sittin' in at one o' them seances?'

'Course not Smudge. But I was wanderin' past the Cemetery the other day and decided t' drop in an' look up me Mum and Dad.

Had t' get one of them curators on the job t' help locate 'em though mind ja.'

'I'd be a bit careful about using the term "droppin in" too loosely if I was you ol' son. They dig them holes pretty deep ya know. One careless step Curly ... that's all it takes!' Smudge chuckled.

'Don't think there was too much in the way o' fresh excavatin' goin' on where I found 'em Smudge. They've been gone f' twenty years now, and I reckon y'd need one o' them jackhammers t' go makin' any impact on the soil mate.'

'Strewth it's not exactly an inspirin' or upliftin' choice o' topic y'd have t' agree though Curl! A bloke doesn't wanna be lingerin' too long over thoughts of the hereafter if y' get me drift.'

'It's only f' a moment or two mate.'

'Ya got it wrong there ol' son. It's f' bloody eternity as far as I can make out.'

'Anyhow Smudge gettin' back t' me original question ... while I was searchin', I noticed this couple cosy as y' please, each settled back in one o' them fold up canvas chairs from Bunnings. Fully equipped they were! Thermos flask 'n wicker basket spread out on the lawn, drinkin' tea an' eatin' a cut lunch of ham 'n pickle sandwiches. Looked t' be havin' a nice ol' time entertainin' themselves 'n chattin' t'gether in the company of their dearly departed while soakin' up the sunshine.

Well it was okay f' them I thought ... at least they were still castin' a shadow. But couldn't help sparin' a second thought f' the poor ol' bugger planted some six feet under who struck me as bein' at a decidedly 'n somewhat unfortunate disadvantage.'

'Not too much communicatin' goin' on in this particular instance by the sound of it Curly!'

'The two sittin' up top musta had a fair bit t' talk about. But the point is Smudge, I woulda considered it a little extreme t' be havin' one o' them tea parties at the Cemetery when a certain ... well you know who ... was missin' out in partakin' of the goodies or contributin' t' the conversation.'

'Fair dinkum it takes all kinds Curly. An' I can think of a lot better places I'd rather have a picnic. Just a touch insensitive if ya askin' my opinion. It's one thing payin' y' respects 'n tendin' the rose bushes, but picnicking beside some poor bastards grave site is really stretchin' the relationship I reckon. What's brought all this on anyway ol' son?'

'Ya gunna think it a bit weird Smudge, but I've received a message from an old friend.'

'There's nothin' weird about that Curly.'

'I reckon ya might be inclined t' change y' mind when I tell ya that she passed away several years ago.'

'Come off it mate ... y'll have t' get up a whole lot earlier in the day before ya can fool an intelligent bloke such as m'self with that sort o' cock 'n bull story!'

'But this is no joke, Smudge.'

'Geez, if that's really the case then Curly, this whole situation as a bloke's bein' led t' understand it, is a bloody disgrace. Ya don't mean t' tell me y' only just now received a letter in the mail that was posted by this friend o' yours sometime prior to her departure all them years ago?'

'Well not exactly Smudge. And it wasn't y' normal type letter. Y' see I switched on me computa the other night and was lookin' through me files, when suddenly I saw the word "Geraldine" printed out in big bold letters. The problem was that I'd never saved a document under that headin'.'

'Maybe y've been visited by one o' them hackers Curly! Once they access ya computa, anythin's possible.'

'It was her Smudge. There's not a doubt in me mind.'

'Who mate?'

'Me friend that died. The one I've just been tellin' ya about. Geraldine Delaney of course. The strange part about it is that a couple o' weeks back, I was out walkin' Shakes, and Geraldine's voice popped int' me mind from outa nowhere. Then I could suddenly pitcha her as a little girl skippin' along the footpath. It was spooky Smudge.'

'Crikey, it sounds like you were hallucinatin' ol' son. A sheila skippin' along the footpath! You've been livin' on ya own f' too long. So didja open up the file then Curly?'

'It was all there! A message apologisin' fer somethin' that happened long ago. Beautiful it was Smudge, and I wanted t' keep readin' it over and over.'

'Fair dinkum mate, y're beginnin' t' even sound like one o' them sheilas the way ya talkin. So what happened next?'

'Well I tried t' print off a copy. But the page kept comin' out blank.'

'What did she say then in the message?'

'She told me that a broken heart can be mended, and good fortune was gunna shine down on me.'

'Since when 'ave you been sufferin' with a broken heart Curly? Are ya sure she's not gettin' ya mixed up with someone else? P'rhaps you were dreamin'.'

'This was no dream Smudge. The followin' mornin' I couldn't wait to read it again. But when I opened up me writin' there was no further trace of it. Geraldine had gone!'

'Ya kiddin' me aren't ya? Ya mean t' say she just up 'n left. Spirited away like some ghost in the night!'

'She did leave the key though Smudge.'

'Ya mean t' say that y' found a key?' Blimey Curly where is it? Can I see it?'

'I can't show anyone Smudge. But at least the lock has now been opened.'

'Well that's a bit of an anti climax wouldn't ya say? What was it that ya unlocked anyway mate?'

'It was somethin' inside me Smudge, that'd been shut down f' a very long time I reckon.'

'Was it somethin' t' do with ya plumbin' then mate? Are ya tryin' t' tell me that some sorta miracle has occurred 'n y've been cured of a life threatenin' condition? Is that why ya had a broken heart?'

'Don't believe that a bloke'd go so far as t' put it in those terms Smudge, but a certain matta had been givin' me some ongoin' concern in a manner of speakin.'

'Well no wonder it's so damned difficult t' communicate with the dead when with all due respect there ol' son, a bloke can't even get through to the livin'. Y' never mentioned a word about this, an' Shaz and I woulda wanted t' know if ya haven't been feelin' up t' ya ol' self there Curly.'

'There's no need t' be worryin' any further mate.'

'If you say so Curly!' And for the second time that day Smudge scratched his head. `But a bloke still can't help gettin' the feelin' that he's missin' the plot here. Is this Geraldine sheila like one o' Mother Mary MacKillop's off siders do y' reckon? How is it that she can send messages on the computa and cure y' illness with the help of some invisible key? Next thing ya know, that gnome y' got sittin' out in the front garden'll be sheddin' real tears of blood for ya Curly an' them pilgrims'll be linin' up outside ya 'ouse.'

'I'll grant ya it's a mystery alright, but there's no need t' go knockin' somethin' just cause ya can't explain it.'

'Well a bloke wouldn't be meanin' any disrespect, but I think ya need t' take it easy 'n get a bit more rest ol' son. It'd seem fairly evident judgin' from this story y've been spinnin' me, that it's all in ya imagination.'

'Geraldine's message was pretty clear Smudge. Yet 'I reckon a good nights sleep wouldn't go astray. So I might just take y' advice an' call it a day.'

A few minutes later as he was on his way out through the back gate, Smudge could have sworn that he heard Curly muttering some strange words. He stopped dead in his tracks for a moment and quietly listened. *What was he on about now? Talkin' to Shakes more than likely.* But whatever he was saying didn't seem to be making a whole lot of sense. Nothing had made sense that day. Curly had been very vague about divulging the details of his exact ailment. *But wait ... there it was again –*

For the third time on that same day Smudge scratched his head, and on this occasion there was no mistaking just exactly what Curly was saying. It was some sort of warning ...

Don't step on a crack or you'll break your mother's back!

That's a bit odd, Smudge thought. *Hadn't Curly just this minute finished tellin' him that his mum had been dead and buried f' nigh on twenty years. It was becomin' more 'n more difficult lately t' work his best mate out.*

In The Doghouse

Curly's eyelids were heavy. He could feel himself nodding off in the chair during the last quarter of the footy, when suddenly, he almost jumped out of his skin at the sound of a loud thumping on the backdoor.

'Okay, okay! Hold y' horses,' Curly shouted above Shakespeare's ferocious barking, whilst somewhat reluctantly making his way across the room.

'Whose out there?' he demanded.

Shakespeare was now frantically scratching and whimpering at the bottom of the door.

'Gawd stone the crows, it's only me Curly, not the flamin' Avon lady callin. Let me in will ya!'

'Bloody hell Smudge ... it's quarta to eleven.' Curly mumbled whilst pulling down the bolt and unfastening the chain to discover Smudge stamping his feet on the mat and blowing into the palm of his hands.

'Fair dinkum, this place is all shut up tighter than Fort Knox. Anyone'd think y' were expectin' Hannibal Lector t' be standin' out here armed with his butcher's knife, 'n just waitin' to chop you up int' palatable sized meaty bites.'

'Geez y' scared the livin' daylights outa me Smudge. What the hell brings y' round rousin' me up at this time o' night?'

'Well excuse me Curly – was a bloke s'posed t' make an appointment or somethin'? Shakes woulda ripped an arm 'n a leg off before lettin' any stranger within coo-ie of you ol' son … wouldn't y' fella?'

Shakespeare's tail whipped back and forth in excitement.

'So what's the problem Smudge … Shaz isn't sick is she?'

'Curly, stop askin' so many questions and lets get in outa this bitin' wind.'

Smudge rushed towards the heater and reached out his hands, rubbing them together. He then turned around to warm his backside.

'Geez are y' workin' on a tight budget here Curly? What settin' have y' got this flamin' heater on anyway? A bloke'd be strugglin' t' warm up his big toe at this rate ol' son.'

'Eighteen degrees Smudge.'

'You need some of them insulatin' bats and some decent blinds mate. Y' heat's disappearing straight out through y' ceilin' 'n between them flimsy excuse f' curtains y' got hangin' on the windows. How about we turn the thermastat up a notch or two 'n pretend we're in the tropics while we watch the end of the footy?'

'Fair go Smudge, a fella's not made of money y' know. Here put this rug around ya.'

'What's up with ya Curly? They only use them things t' keep the old peoples' legs warm in the Nursin' Home. I'm not a geriatric yet y' know. But t' tell y' the truth a bloke could easily freeze t' death on a night like this, 'n who d' ya reckon'd give a stuff? Not a single solitary soul. Me life is just meanin'less. Did ja hear me Curly ... meanin'less!'

'That's a bit rough mate ... lots o' people'd be worrying if anythin' happened to you, includin' me 'n Shakes here.'

'Well at least that's nice of y' t' say ol' son. But the way that Shaz carrys on sometimes, anyone'd think a bloke's the village idiot. Kicked me outa the house she did. Kicked me outa me own house on a night that's not fit f' man or beast. A bloke's home is s'posed to be his castle Curly. I've worked 'n slaved t' keep a roof over me missus' head, and this is all the thanks I get f' bustin' me boiler. Scrimpin' 'n savin' t' pay the bloody bills mate.'

'Aw don't worry Smudge, I'm sure if Shaz is upset with ya, that it'll all blow over by the mornin'. You've had y' blues before I reckon.'

'Too right we have ... but this is different Curly! A bloke can only take so much, and this time she's pushed me too far. There'll be no goin' back ... not on y' life ol' son. An' you being me best mate 'n all, I was wonderin if I could shack up with ya f' a night or two just till I can get m'self settled?'

'No worries Smudge. Y're welcome t' stay as long as y' like … you know that.'

'Bloody decent of y' Curly. A bloke'll be filin' f' divorce within the week the way things are shapin' up, so I'll be lookin' around f' me own digs and a bit of independence. Then we'll find out how she manages without me 'round t' take care of 'er.'

'What about I boil up the billy 'n when you get a bit of shut eye, everythin'll look a whole lot rosier t'morrow.'

'Rosier Curly! D' y' reckon this is some sort of a walk in the park? A bloody garden party or somethin'! I'm disappointed in y' attitude sometimes ol' son, 'n besides surely you can't be thinkin' a blokes on the wagon, just because I've split up with me Missus. A cup o' bloody tea is f' sheilas mate. Hand me one o' them cans outta the fridge will ya.'

'It's a bit late to be drownin' y' sorrows at this time of night. Anyway me 'n Shakes are off t' bed, so make y'self at home in the spare room. You know where t' find everythin'.'

'Well don't let a little hiccup such as y' best mates marital breakdown keep y' up all night worryin' Curly. At the time a bloke most needs t' bend y' ear, y' just up 'n leave him sittin' here like a shag on a rock freezin' me flamin' rear end off.'

'Sorry Smudge, but I reckon me race has been run.'

Curly heard Smudge still stumbling around at midnight, and when he got up the next morning there were six empty cans on the floor, and loud snoring coming from the bedroom. It was not until after eleven that Smudge finally appeared at the kitchen doorway, blowing his nose into one of Curly's hand towels.

'Think I'm comin' down with a wog on top of all me troubles.'

'Gee that's no good Smudge. Maybe you should go back t' bed for a while!'

'But what's f' brekkie ol' son ... a bit o' bubble 'n squeak?'

'Shakes 'n I have had breakfast three hours ago mate 'n are just on our way out f' a walk. But y're welcome t' make y'self some toast 'n vegemite.'

'Toast 'n vegemite! What sort of a meal d' y' call that Curly? Shaz always makes me bacon 'n eggs whenever I'm feelin' a bit below par.'

'Sorry mate, I haven't done me shoppin'. Maybe y' might like t' tag along with me later 'n push the trolley!'

'Y're got t' be kiddin' me Curly. Ya won't catch me inside one o' them Supermarkets in a hurry. Shaz does all the shoppin' at our place.'

'Hang on a minute will y' Smudge, there's the phone ringin'.'

'Don't answer it Curl. It'll be Shaz beggin' me to come home, I'll guarantee it mate. It's downright embarrassin' hearin' her grovellin' like that.'

'Hello,' Curly answered, 'yep ... okay ... sure ... '

In The Doghouse

'Well what did she say Curly?'

'It was one of the neighbours Smudge wanting me to collect his mail while he's away next week. But I'm certain Shaz'll be in touch, just to check that y're okay. See ya when we get back from our walk.'

Later when Curly returned there was no sign of Smudge, just a quickly scribbled note on the kitchen table – *Curly, what did I tell ya. Shaz called while you were out and was cryin' 'n pleadin' with me t' come home. Naturally I told her there was no point in trying t' get around me ...'*

Curly dialed Smudge's number – 'G'day Shaz ... has Smudge arrived home yet?'

'He better not show his face around here if he knows what's good for him Curly O'Callahan.'

Geez things are serious when Shaz starts callin' me by me full name. Curly thought.

'Well I think he's on his way Shaz, so go easy on the ol' bugger! He's always so miserable whenever you get mad at him, and he really can't manage without you, y' know.'

'Yes right! Well we'll see about that now won't we Curly? S'pose he's called on your help to try and soften me up has he?'

'Are ya there Luv?' Curly heard Smudge's, butter wouldn't melt in the mouth, muffled voice in the background.

'For God's sake, he's just walking up the pathway armed with the largest bunch of roses you've ever seen. That must have hurt!

Smudge hates spending his money on unnecessary ... Better go Curly.'

'These marital tiffs are always a problem Shakes,' Curly sighed as he put the phone down. 'Let's just hope that all's forgiven. Much 'n all as I love me mate Smudge, I hate t' say it, but just don't think we were meant t' live together.'

Why Curly Writes

It was the end of third term and Curly hadn't written a word for several weeks. He'd been far too busy sorting through folders in search of the best of his work to include in the upcoming edition of the annual "Anthology".

'What d' ya reckon about this story then Smudge?'

'Geez Curly ... watch out f' a bloke's beer mate. Y' nearly knocked me can flyin' arse over head with all them great mess o' papers.

'Aw sorry Smudge. I'm not quite meself at the moment.'

'Now settle down mate ... there's no need f' gettin' all worked up about nothin'. An' correct me if I'm wrong Curly, but takin' int' account all that y've already told me, as a bloke now sees it, these 'ere booklets aren't exactly gunna be circulatin' throughout the masses. So what I'd like t' know is ... what's all the fuss about? I reckon y' should just stick in a couple of y' favourites and be done with it. Here ... hand 'em all over t' me mate. Eeny, meeny, miny, mo ...'

Curly snatched the pages back out of Smudge's hands in disgust.

'Well they may not be distributed amongst the masses as y' say Smudge. But that's no reason to treat me contribution lightly. A bloke's gotta take pride in 'is work and think this matter through carefully. After all, it's not every day o' the week a writer gets the chance t' be published.'

'Whose gunna read 'em ol' son?'

'There could be up t' as many as fifty people thumbin' through the pages at any one time Smudge.'

'Fifty! That's bugger all Curly. Whose ya distributin' agent? We need to get y' a wider circle o' readers than that. I'll tell ya what we'll do! How about you 'n me buy up a hundred copies of this 'ere "andrology" and sell 'em off at the pub. The bloke's 'd be more than happy to chip in an' support a good cause.'

'It's an "anthology" Smudge. An' no one's lookin' f' charity. I want me audience t' be fair dinkum interested in what they're gunna be readin', 'n t' appreciate the quality of all me friends' great writin'. The last thing I need is f' them fellas at the pub t' be spillin' their beer all over the front covers.'

'Maybe we could raffle 'em off in rolled up bundles and stick a few inside them Xmas hampers. That way they'll be kept in mint condition 'n well outa harms way. No direct contact an' unnecessary handlin' of the goods ol' son. Y' can imagine a bloke's missus 'd love t' read some o' them romantic poems 'n share 'em 'round amongst 'er girlfriends. Ya know what these sheilas are like Curly!'

'Forget about whose gunna' be buyin' 'em Smudge. That's not me problem. F' all I know there could be a mob o' customers waitin' in line just fightin' t' get their hands on the very first copy hot off the printin' press. In fact, they might even be campin' out overnight on the footy oval equipped with their eskies an' thermos flasks. But all I'm askin' at this stage is some help to sort out a couple o' me best pieces.'

'Well Curly ... why do y' write mate? That's the sixty-four dollar question! Once y' settle that score in y' mind – y've got ya answer. These days, Eddie Mcguire 'd be offerin' y' a cool million t' ring an intelligent friend such as meself. Someone well qualified t' assist ya in seekin' out this type o' privileged information.'

'How does that work Smudge?'

'Y' gotta be kiddin' me brother. Shaz won't believe it. Every man 'n 'is dog musta watched that show.'

'Of course I've seen it Smudge. I was talkin' about y' question. Somethin' to do with why I write.'

'It's simple Curly. Just pick out a story which pretty much sums up ya reason f' writin'.

'Surprisin'ly enough, that seems like pretty sound advice I reckon Smudge.'

'Course it's sound advice. When have I ever given ya a bum steer Curly?'

'Crikey, now that y' come t' mention it Smudge. Y're absolutely right.'

'Okay Curl, since we've got that one all sorted, let's consida y're options. What is it that y' like best about writin'? An' as y' not a contestant mate, y' don't even need t' lock in either A, B, C or D!'

'Well, I think it's been findin' me own voice Smudge ... and havin' it heard by me friends at the writin' group.'

'Good start ol' son. What else?'

'Makin' 'em laugh mate. It's all about reachin' out an' touchin' another through the power of words that I've found so satisfyin'.'

'There y' have it Curly. Which story did they like the best?'

'I can't rememba!'

'This is the tricky part where a trusted friend can be called upon f' some much valued advice. An' fortunately for you Curly ... I'm ya man! So what d' ya reckon of the one y' wrote almost first up? Somethin' about pickin' up an infection.'

'That's it Smudge! Y're a bloody genius mate and a lifesaver t'boot.'

'Well just rememba whose been y' chief advisor when y' work becomes famous Curly. The bloke who did all the ground work and got ya started so t' speak. An' Curly, don't forget t' order plenty 'o copies and invite Shaz an' meself along to the big andrology launch. We'll be the good lookin' pair in the front row cheerin' the loudest for ya ol' son.'

The Curly O'Callahan School Of Hard Knocks

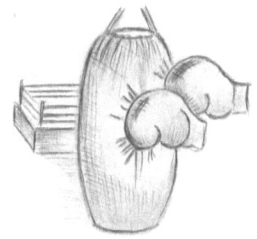

'What's that y're jottin' down there in y' notebook Curly?'

'This here's me "Ode to the Slap" Smudge.'

'I reckon I've heard about that book Curly. Shaz has been watchin' the series on TV. Let me read ya poem there will ya. A bloke'd be interested in hearin' what y' got t' say concernin' this extremely contentious matter.' Curly handed over his notepad and watched Smudge's face carefully to try and gauge his reaction.

'Geez ... ya can't go around writin' stuff like this mate. A bloke could get "life" f' even thinkin' these words, let alone listin' 'em down on paper'. Criminal intent they'd charge y' with! An accessory t' child brutality! Incitin' the reader t' commit an unlawful act! An' the list goes on. We're no longer livin' back in the dark ages. We're a civilised society ol' son. Hasn't anybody bothered t' enlighten ya.'

'Think I'm willin' t' take me chances there Smudge. Just a bit of a play on words really more than anythin' else. Sparin' the rod an' spoilin' the child is written with a tongue in cheek approach. The reader can make up his own mind.'

"Foot in mouth approach" might be a little more t' the point I reckon there, Curl!'

'Is there anythin' I left off the list then Smudge?'

'Crikey Curly ... y're gotta be jokin'? Talk about diggin' y'self a deeper hole. But I do recollect that accordin' t' me ol' man, 'e never could go too far wrong in providin' us kids with an occasional good, swift "foot up the backside". He considered this t' be one of his all time favourites, 'n a bloke's still nursin' some of the bruises t' prove it.'

'Well p'rhaps kickin' might be pushin' the boundaries a bit I s'pose Smudge, considerin' a slap is so frowned on.'

'No matter what y' opinion might be Curly if y're thinkin' about actin' within the law, the boundary is very clear. An' by t'days standards it seems the worst that can happen t' most of them kids when they start playin' up, is about as serious as an empty threat deprivin' 'em of their favourite flavour when pickin' out one o' them lollipops.'

'Come off it Smudge. Don't ya know that kids aren't allowed t' eat too many sweets these days. It turns 'em int' regular psychopaths mate. They become uncontrollable and start tearin' around shoutin' 'n screamin' after only as little as a few grains o' sugar.'

'Fair dinkum Curly, times 'ave changed and they just keep on changin' with each generation. A bloke'd be the first t' agree that nowadays somethin' pertainin' t' them finer social graces certainly seems to be lackin'. It's all about the age ol' art o' simple good manners and havin' a bit o' respect f' ya neighbour. So the way I see it Curly, is even though we all hate takin' our unpleasant tastin' medicine, there's no denyin' the fact that it helps us t' recover in the long run ... now doesn't it mate?'

'So ya reckon a slap's okay then do ya Smudge?'

'Funny! I can't recall sayin' that exactly ... now can I Curly?'

'The Slap'

The slap, the strap, the smack, the whack – will surely get him back on track.

The box, the hit, the clip, the cuff – no longer shall he be so tough.

The spank, the lash, the wallop, the clout – will leave him in no further doubt.

The slug, the strike, the sock, the blow – then no more tantrums should he throw.

The belt, the bang, the clobber, the bash – the house he shall not dare to trash.

The jab, the biff, the punch, the thump – shall squarely sit him on his rump.

The tap, the knock, the push, the shove – he's now a child you're proud to love.

The Curly O'Callahan School of Hard Knocks.

The Royal Handbag

'Have you ever given' any consideration t' writin' one o' them memwahs Curly?'

'Nah not really Smudge. People might think that a bloke was skitin' or somethin'.'

'Strewth what in the flamin' hell would y' be skitin' about?'

'Well f' instance, you recall that time I got t' meet 'er Majesty don't y' Smudge? How d' y' reckon that'd go down with me mates at the pub?'

'Hadn't really crossed me mind ol' son. S'pose it's not every day that y' average Joe Blow finds 'imself lunchin' in the company of royalty. But y' never have told me what she 'ad t' say t' ya exactly.'

'She didn't say nothin' really Smudge. Some bloke wearin' one o' them fancy outfits ... the Gov'na's aide I reckon ya might call 'im, more or less warned us t' keep our mouths shut. Unless 'er Majesty speaks to ya first, he says, don't even think about tryin' t' entice her int' chattin'.'

'D' y' reckon she'd actually remember ya though if you were to run inta 'er again at the Buckin'ham pub or somewhere?'

'Nup, it's a bit disappointin' mate, but there'd be absolutely no chance. When each of us had our turn, the sheilas got t' do a little curtesy affair 'n the blokes bowed their 'eads, then with a squiz 'n a hand shake it was all over as quick as winkin'.'

'Well Curly, I'd be includin' that in me life story if I was you. Afterall y' knock about bloke in the street wouldn't have a clue about this kinda stuff. It's important t' know just what's goin' through the mind o' the monarch, 'n not many people 'ave had first 'and knowledge of this sorta privileged information.'

But I couldn't really tell ya what she was thinkin' Smudge.'

'Doesn't matter ol' son, just make it up as ya go along. No one's gunna be none the wiser. If I was you, I'd be tellin' y' readers that y' sat right next t' 'er an' got chattin' about Camilla 'n Charlie. Maybe you coulda' been comparin' notes about the corgis an' ol' Shakes 'ere, or what she likes t' carry around in them han'bags she always got slung over 'er arm.'

'She just carries 'er hankie and a bit o' lippy like any other sheila, I reckon.'

'Aw turn it up Curly, how can ya be so certain? Have you ever seen 'er blowin' 'er hoota or caught her reapplyin' her lippy? Not in ya life mate. Royalty just don't do them things in public. It's beneath 'em ol' son. Then they'd start lookin' like the rest o' us commoners, 'n that's why they've got all them servants to blow their noses for 'em. So I'm tellin' ya Curly she could well have somethin' really surprisin' inside them han'bags. This is the sorta stuff ya gotta work on. Somethin' interestin' 'n original that might be a bit compellin' to the reader ... somethin' that no one'll be expectin'.'

'That could be a bit tricky. Y' can't just go makin' up stuff ya know.'

'Geez writers make up stuff all the time 'n a little bit of embellishment in all the right places doesn't do anyone any harm. Besides all them other authors can talk about is them royal sex scandals. I reckon everyone's sick o' hearin' that same ol' rubbish, n' someone bright such as y'self needs t' take a long hard look at things from a bit of a different angle.'

'Well wha' d' you reckon she's got in them han'bags then Smudge?'

'You think about it Curly, she takes 'em everywhere with 'er whether she's walkin' round in the Palace, or even gettin' them por-trates painted. Who else that y' can think of carries their han'bag all around the house with 'em. It's unnatural I tell ya mate 'n it wouldn't at all surprise me if she tucks one that matches 'er nightie under the blanket when she goes t' bed. I reckon she's got a problem Curly like them possessive compulsive people that keep checkin' t' see if they've switched off the iron. There could be nothin' at all in them han'bags, but then again if you can come up with the correct answer, you could be a very rich man one day.'

'You mean obsessive compulsive I think Smudge.'

'Makes not a scrap o' difference Curly! Possessive, obsessive, there's no point splittin' hairs when it's all boiled down.

'Maybe it's just 'er medication? She's gotta have her private moments Smudge, and that's when she prob'ly blows her hoota 'n powders 'er nose mate.'

'Don't you believe it. I'm tellin' ya there's somethin' more goin' on with them han'bags than meets the eye.'

'Crikey, I reckon y' makin' a mountain outa a molehill. How the hell do I know what she's carryin' around inside her flamin' han'bag, n' apart from you Smudge I'm not so sure who really gives a bugger?'

'I dunno Curly ... a bloke tries 'is hardest t' expand y' horizons 'n broaden y' intellect with somethin' a little bit challengin' an' outa the ordin'ry and what sorta thanks do I get? If y' want my advice forget about them run o' the mill paperartzi stories ... treat it like a little test o' sorts. Now good luck ol' son and start writin' them memwahs. I'll be keen t' see just what y' come up with!'

Jingle Bells

'Got ya Christmas tree up yet Curly?'

'Fair go Smudge ... it's only Novemba.'

'Well Shaz is already tackin' up them garlands all over the 'ouse. Makes the place look untidy if ya ask me.   I tell ya Curly, by the time she gets through decoratin', there's not a space left anywhere t' safely put ya beer down without losin' it in amongst all them baubles 'n pine cones. A bloke becomes delusional thinkin' he's Santa Claus himself livin' out the next two months surrounded by flamin' tinsel.

'Aw ... it's all pretty harmless I reckon Smudge, 'n Christmas is kinda special. Shaz gets a kick out o' puttin' her stamp on things. Speakin' o' which ... a bloke auta be headin' off t' the Post Office next time I'm up at the shoppin' centa, an' stockin' up on a few packs o' them special greetin' cards with the kookaburrras on 'em before they all sell out.'

'Not them ones with the shacks 'n gum trees again Curly? What the hell 'ave they got t' do with Christmas?'

'They're me favourites Smudge!'

'S'pose you'll be sendin' one off t' that Penny-lope sheila this year! But don't reckon she'd go f' them kookaburras in too much of a hurry though Curly ... her bein' of Spanish extraction y' understand. A bloke'd be needin' t' fork out a bit extra 'an shoutin' y'self one o' them more upmarket 'allmark type cards. Somethin' with a meanin'ful verse 'n a bit o' that twinklin' snow on the front.'

'Crikey Smudge. I'm not plannin' on spendin' six bucks on one Christmas card if that's what ya suggestin' ... even f' you mate.'

'Well that's a bit bloody disappointin' Curly. I woulda thought ya best mate meant more t' ya than that.

'Maybe I'll send ya the one with the cockatoos then.'

'Don't go puttin' y'self out or anythin' ol' son ... them cockatoos bein' so difficult t' part with 'n all.'

'It's nothin' really Smudge!'

'But ya know what, Curly, all this talkin' about the silly season has just reminded me ... wouldja believe them neighbours up the street are fittin' out their entire place with all them reindeers 'n fairy lights again. I reckon ya coulda seen that house from outa space last Christmas. Bloody amazin' it was!'

'It's all the go mate. Didja ever see that pitcha about Christmas with the Griswalds? Chevy Chase really outdid 'imself. I remember them family of chipmunks were still nestin' in the tree, when he stood it up in his hallway. Can't get anythin' more authentic than that Smudge!'

'Well I'll tell ya one bloke that doesn't wanna bar o' this Chevy Chase caper. It won't be happenin' at our place Curly. I've told Shaz she's gotta stop spendin' on all them extravagant blow up Santas. Every five minutes she's in an' out o' them Reject Shops. A bloke can't be expected t' go climbin' up on the roof at my age, tyin' down inflatable sleighs 'n cardboard cut outs ont' the chimney. A decent puff o' wind Curly, 'n the whole lot'll finish up somewhere driftin' south o' the flamin' North Pole.'

'Everyone's doin' it now Smudge. Me 'n Shakes go walkin' in the dark durin' December, just t' check out all them lights 'round the neighbourhood.'

'Blimey Curly, it's blokes like you that encourage this sorta nonsense. Where's it gunna end? When I was a kid we made do with them hand-made paper chains strung across the ceilin'.'

'Well I reckon one o' them pine trees'll do the job f' meself 'n Shakes as usual.'

'I'm warnin' ya ol' son, ya better get in early, cause Shaz always picks out the cream o' the crop. She goes over them pine trees with a fine tooth comb, carefully inspectin' each one individually, while agonizin' over the shape of every branch. Let me tell ya Curly that Shaz is the queen o' the original Christmas tree pickers. It's bloody embarrassin' mate! Ends up buyin' one that's twelve foot tall. Then ol' muggins here has t' saw off the bottom t' get it inside the door.'

'Ya gotta admit it's a bit o' fun I s'pose Smudge. We're all still kid's at heart, so why not make the most of it?'

'It's costin' me an arm 'n a leg that's why Curly.'

'Where's ya Christmas spirit Smudge? Remember Scrooge? Ya almost startin' t' sound like him.'

'Awright mate … I get ya drift, but that's just downright insultin' to go implyin' a bloke is mean.'

'What are y' talkin' about Smudge?'

'This year, let the record show, that ol' Smudge here is an extremely generous fella. A bloke doesn't take too kindly t' them deflamator-ial accusations about bein' a miser Curly. It's bloody hurtful ol' son. So y've just this minute convinced me that Shaz is gunna be haulin' away the tallest tree that she can lay 'er 'ands on. It'll be so large, that she'll be needin' t' hire one o' them semi trailers just t' deliver it.'

'But that's stupid mate. How are y' gunna fit an even bigger tree int' the lounge room?'

'No worries Curl. I've got it all sorted. We'll stick it out in the middle of the front lawn. It'll be ablaze with a thousand light bulbs. Remember that Curly … one thousand! And a bloke might even go truckin' in a load o' that special snow, 'n consida settin' up an entire forest. Whatever happens … there'll be no scrimpin'!'

'Blimey, that's a bit of a sudden about turn wouldn't ya say mate? Have ya really thought this whole thing through?'

'Curly, the only real thinkin' that needs doin' is f' you 'n Shakes t' be re-directin' ya walkin' route ol' son. Cause I'm tellin' ya right now … Christmas has just arrived in Smudgeville!'

Morning Writing Revisited

Curly's special writing year would shortly be drawing to a close. And as he completed the final sentence of the last story for his class of 2011, he was of course, already one step ahead, contemplating what tales he might wish to produce in the future. But during the past months ... hadn't Curly forgotten something? What had happened to the writing bug? After all, it was the writing bug that had initially prompted this story to begin.

Curly now shut down his computer – the morning having already ended. `Shakes ... I reckon it's time f' a stroll.' You may think that little has changed. But Curly knows better. Throughout the course of the preceding months, so much had changed. Yet perhaps so few, apart from himself, may have noticed.

Shakespeare leapt up and raced into the bedroom to find Curly's walking shoes. He picked the left one up in his mouth and brought it back to drop at Curly's feet. He then returned and sniffed out the right shoe wedged beneath the chest of draws. Gripping the shoelaces firmly between his teeth, slowly he dragged it free.

As they set off at a quiet pace along the street, Curly noticed his neighbour, old Charlie Coglan, in the distance. It was too late to turn back or try and conceal himself amongst the bushes.

'G'day Curly! Haven't seen ya round much lately. How's ya bins holdin' up these days,' he mischievously chuckled. `Any space left inside 'em? Was hopin' ya might help a bloke out with some of me excess bottles!'

'There's no need f' being sarcastic an' makin' fun o' me Charlie. But if ya really wanna know, me bins are still brimmin' over with rubbish. Kinda strange, considerin' that me n' Shakes here are livin' on our own don't ya reckon? An' even stranger seein' as how Nellie's now outa action.'

'It wouldn't at all surprise me if Nellie's been roamin' the neighbourhood again ya know Curly, even though she's s'posed to have some sorta carer lookin' after 'er.'

'Well it's a cryin' shame about Nellie. But there's no point blamin' 'er or wastin' me time by resurrectin' the past 'n discussin' this annoyin' habit any further. So let's just drop the subject will we!'

'Sounds t' me like y've gone a bit soft on it there Curly.'

'Fair dinkum Charlie ... ya never know when it's time t' let up on a bloke, now do ya?'

But it was at this point that the conversation took a sudden turn and Curly became aware of something, which he'd long forgotten.

'Hey, is that a bug on ya shoulder there, Curly?'

'What the hell are ya talkin' about?' Curly asked as he brushed his hand across the top of his shirt sleeve.

'I tell ya there's a bloody bug sittin' right there on ya shoulder. Looks like one o' them ladybirds. Aren't they s'posed t' be a sign o' good luck, or money, or somethin'? So I wouldn't go gettin' too upset about it all Curly.'

'Whose gettin' upset about it! Anyone'd think a bloke's some sorta snivellin' sheila the way you carry on Charlie Coglan.'

For some unknown reason, Charlie had always managed to rub Curly up the wrong way and bring out the worst in his normally easy going manner. This bloke had somehow mastered the knack of making him feel perpetually grumpy.

'Come on then Shakes, we need t' get movin' if we're gunna be back in time t' watch the news mate.'

'Suit y'self O'Callahan. Don't go lettin' me hold ya up or nothin'. A bloke wouldn't wanna be accused of intrudin' on ya many important commitments or anythin'.'

Curly ignored him and quickened his step, rounding the corner before Charlie had the chance to bail him up again. Ever since that embarrassing bin episode, he had gone out of his way to try and avoid ole Cogs. But until this very moment Curly hadn't really given a thought to the bug he'd complained of at the start of the year.

'Crikey Shakes ... cast ya mind back f' a bit and ya may remember when I was worried about havin' some sort of an infection?' Shakespeare turned his head and lifted his wispy brows up to expose two rounded eyes, which now came to rest on Curly's face. `Well that Charlie Coglan's not good f' much I reckon, but at least he's just alerted a bloke t' the fact that I've been carryin' this same bug around with me f' all that time n' entirely forgotten about it. Only now have I come t' realise that it's completely harmless mate. The writin' bug is harmless, 'n I don't care anymore if I never get rid of it. I wanna keep writin' fer the rest of me days Shakes.'

Shakespeare responded with a joyful woof. If only he could have explained that to Curly right back at the very beginning. They continued along the pathway in companionable silence, the man and his beloved dog, then finally turned and headed for home.

The writing bug followed ...

About the Author

Colleen has explored many creative pursuits in her lifetime. At 62, she began writing her family memoir (as yet unpublished), 'Journey to Johanna', completing it a year later.

Colleen and her husband, Bill, have lived in Greensborough, Victoria for forty-five years. They have two married children and four grandchildren. *The Curly Collection* is her first published book and she hints that a sequel is possible. Colleen's greatest literary ambition is to write a serious novel.